Rhonda Bartle was born in New Plymouth in 1954. *The Lie of the Land* is her second published novel, and was the winner of the 2003 Richard Webster Popular Fiction Award. In 1999 Bartle won the BNZ Katherine Mansfield Award with an excerpt from her first novel *The Gospel @ccording to Cole* which was published in 2000.

Also by Rhonda Bartle

The Gospel @ccording to Cole (Cape Catley, 2000)

What reviewers said about *The Gospel @ccording to Cole:*

"Clever, poetic, very readable – a play around human emotions and a search for some meaning to life… Brief and brilliant."
– Hawke's Bay Today

"Bartle's strength is believable, endearing and well-drawn characters. Her writing is witty, fresh and snappy, with a sharp eye for the scenes of family life."
– Sunday Star Times

"Bartle gets it right with unforced wit and keen observation."
– Wairarapa Times-Age

"…wry, funny, clever and packed with modern day angst. [*The Gospel @ccording to Cole*] reads so much like real life, it needs the author's disclaimer at the front to reassure the reader that it isn't."
– The Northern Advocate

The Lie of the Land

Rhonda Bartle

HAZARD PRESS
publishers

For the boys

Acknowledgements

Grateful thanks to Creative New Zealand for funding.

The quote on p. 124 and the song of welcome on p. 139 are both from *Oriori* by Robyn Kahukiwa and Roma Potiki.

Published by Hazard Press Limited
P.O. Box 2151, Christchurch, New Zealand
Email: info@hazard.co.nz
www.hazardpress.com

ISBN 1-877270-81-4

Cover painting: *Sky/Feathers: Palliser Bay* oil painting by Rosemary Mortimer reproduced with the kind permission of the artist.

Printed in New Zealand by Astra Print Ltd

What lies behind us, and what lies
before us, are tiny matters –
compared to what lies within us.

Ralph Waldo Emerson

Chapter One

It shouldn't have made any difference who answered the phone that day but for a long time afterwards, it did. It was me, and it was right that it should be me, and not Ty or Charity. Because Ty would have scuffed at the counter with his Nikes, and Charity might have picked at her nails as she tried to get a glimpse of herself in the microwave, wearing the most attentive expression she could manage.

But when the phone rang, I was closest. It's a wonder I heard it over the music being belted out upstairs. I took the phone through to the laundry where it was quieter and sat on the dryer next to the tub, my feet in the Gran's Remedy spilt on the floor. Damn Ty. So concerned about appearing clean but he never did clean up. At sixteen he waltzed around as though I was the slave put on earth to sweep up behind him. Charity was no better. She had thrown her new shirt, the one that had cost a fortune, the one that 'I just have to have or I'll die', into the tub with the dirty tea towels where the tap dripped steadily on them, making no class distinction.

'Cass? Is that you, Cass? This is Beth. Beth Conaglen. Rick's sister.'

My brain repeated 'Rick's sister' like a bad echo.

'It's been a long time, I know. And it's not good news.' And then there was soft nervous laughter as though she understood that her bad news might be something else for me. I imagined her squaring her strong shoulders, preparing to bite the bullet. Just say it.

'Cass, Rick is dead.' Not a bullet I was expecting.

I didn't know what I should feel at that moment, except shot. For a second I didn't feel anything at all until the face of a small brown boy swam into my vision and stuck itself on the wall of my laundry. Leo. My son. And Rick's.

'We need to contact Leo and let him know,' Beth said. 'We don't know where he is. Rick lost track.'

And suddenly I knew what was coming next and I desperately wanted to stop it.

'They haven't…hadn't seen each other…' And then Beth did stop as though she'd heard me.

Thank you, I thought. I'd fill in the gaps myself. Someone had once called me Polly Filler as a joke. I had the habit of finishing other people's sentences without permission. It wasn't much of a talent. I got things wrong even when I desperately wanted to be right. Seen each other since Christmas…since Leo was up at Easter…since the weekend before last…

But just like silly putty, the words went back into the shape they were always going to be when Beth first opened her mouth.

'Well, they hadn't seen each other for a very long time,' she said quietly.

A very long time. My heart turned to liquid and ran into the tub where it soaked Charity's good shirt for a second time. Just like Leo and me, I thought. Only we hadn't seen each other for longer than that. We hadn't seen each other for two lifetimes.

And if I'd been just some distant relative, I might have hung up the phone then wandered through to the kitchen, put my coffee cup into the dishwasher the way I did every day before I went off to sell houses I didn't like to people I didn't like. But I was related to Beth in the worst possible way. We were united by the suffering her brother had caused, which didn't bind us and never could. I remembered something kind she had said to me at the time. 'We all know how much you loved him.' Of course. Mothers love their sons. But even then I had recognised that her words were in the past tense. Loved.

We weren't related, Beth and I, because Rick and I had never been married. We'd had a baby together and that was all. That was all?

'Rick was killed in a head-on. I'm sorry, Cass.' Beth took a small, shuddering breath. Rick was her brother and she had cause to grieve, but I was watching that small familiar face shiver and shine on the wall in front of me. I had cause to grieve too, but not for Rick. Never Rick.

'You probably don't need details, Cass,' Beth said.

'Yes,' I said. 'Give me details.'

Tell me how he put his feet to the floor to stave off the impact and his flesh peeled back so only bones were left. They say if you see the crash coming, you put your feet down to try to stop it. It's instinctive but it doesn't work. I know someone who's a policeman. He says it happens more times than you'd expect. That's real separation for you, Beth, I thought. The separation of flesh from bones, just like a son from his mother.

'Say something comforting,' I said under my breath. Tell me how his head went through the windscreen, that he was unrecognisable when they scraped him from the road. Tell me anything you like because nothing you say about Rick's death can touch me.

'They say he didn't suffer. That he died at the scene.'

Except that.

Leo's blue eyes looked for me through the haze. You don't understand, I told him. I know he was your father but I've hated him for years, on your behalf and mine. I'm not prepared to cry for him now. Anyway, it would take a lot more than Rick's dying to do it. The doctors took part of my body away and all I felt was resigned. Perhaps we're all given just so many tears to cry in a lifetime, I thought, before we all run dry. I ran dry such a long time ago, Leo, there's not even the river bed left. I hope he rots in hell.

I didn't care how it sounded, even in my thoughts. There weren't enough clichés to cover how I felt. I hope he died a thousand deaths, every one of them searing. Had he taken Leo from me all those years ago so someone I barely remembered could ring me up one morning and say, 'They hadn't seen each other for a very long time…'? Now I had extra years to add to the tally. Leo's. I looked at his face on the wall and he was crying.

'I just thought of something,' I said into the phone, into the silence.

'I saw you once, Beth. Afterwards. In the supermarket in Gain Street. You were coming down the aisle towards me. I knew it was you and I couldn't stand it. I left. I parked my trolley next to the bread and walked right out the door. I never went back to that supermarket again. Isn't that funny?' I had a picture then, of the half-filled trolley waiting under the Molenberg sign for my return, the way I'd waited on my mother's porch for my baby. 'I swore I'd never speak to any of you again.'

But I had, I'd broken my own vow. Whenever I'd felt overwhelmed by sadness, I'd pick up the phone and call anyone remotely in control. 'Do you know where Rick is? Where he took my boy?' And before I shattered into a million barbed pieces, or the person on the other end lapsed into terrifying, pointless sympathy, one of us would have enough sense of shame to hang up.

'I always wished we could have stayed friends,' Beth said. 'If it's any consolation, Cass, I didn't like what my brother did, none of us did. But you know Rick. So arbitrary. Black was black and white was white and he was always right. No arguments. Then it was…'

I filled in the gaps again. 'Over. Leo was gone.'

'It was so terrible, I felt so sorry for you,' Beth said. 'Anyway…' stronger now, as though she'd thrown off some history and pulled on the present instead, 'someone heard Leo was living down Wellington way. By the sea. He'd never be far from the sea, now would he?'

I was glad that someone else remembered at least that much about a small boy from Pirongia. I'd often joked in the old days how he must have been born with sand in his bones instead of marrow, like a strange kind of christening present from one of Neptune's clan. He had an affinity with the sea and the creatures in it. Not born with a silver spoon, my Leo, but West Coast iron sand.

The image of Leo vanished – became nothing more than steam from a pot when you ram home the lid. I'd been seeing him as a baby. Then I saw him as a boy. Now, as I sat up straighter and leaned my head on the wall, right arm crossed over my left breast where it always seemed to go, I knew he wasn't even a boy.

'Well, I guess it's more the Wairarapa,' Beth continued. 'Palliser

Bay, they said. Where all those fishermen live.'

I'd read of Palliser Bay. It had the reputation of being as fierce as the coast of Scotland. I'd seen photos of Ngawi, where rusting bulldozers lined the shore like a collection of Funho vehicles in the biggest sandpit in town. It had made a huge impression on me, that something as ugly and as useless-looking as a bulldozer past its use-by date could still be an asset. As necessary to the fishing industry as the boats and pots and the nets. I'd found an unsettling kind of paradox between that and getting old in the city, where even selling real estate required a well-cut suit, good legs and a trendy-coloured lipstick.

I'd never been to Ngawi or anywhere else down there. It had looked a different country, not at all like Auckland where I lived. It was a savage coast with a rugged climate. There were black rocks and huge seas, coves so deep you could launch a proper fishing boat right off the beach. Only a fisherman would choose to live there. Leo would choose to live there. My heart began to thump beneath my palm.

'Beth? Who told you this? Did they say anything else?'

'No. Someone heard it through someone else, who heard it through the grapevine. You know how these things go.'

Yes. I knew how these things go. Someone talked of a sly kiss at last week's party and the information rolled all the way back to me. My husband and Julie Weston. I didn't want to think about it.

'Okay. Thanks. And about Rick. I'm sorry for you and your family,' I said, as sincerely as I could.

'I guess I should let you go now,' Beth said. 'It was a long shot, but I just thought you and Leo might have crossed paths.'

Like two old lovers in a movie theatre? Like two old drunks in a pub?

'How old would he be now?' she asked, and I felt myself slipping, sliding down a yellow laundry wall. I could drown in the tub if I didn't watch out.

'I hate you for your idle curiosity,' I said.

'Don't,' Beth whispered.

But I didn't need a meter ticking inside me to add up the years.

Ask any mother who has lost a child, through any reason, how old that child is now, and she will know.

'Thirty. Thirty years old in August.'

Leo the lion, named for the sign under which he was born. Leos were meant to be sunny personalities, or so Linda Goodman's book of star signs said, and it wasn't wrong. Leo had been born on the edge of a sunny spring.

'My God,' Beth said. 'I guess he must be.'

'Yes,' I said. 'My God.' The sand had trickled through the hourglass without anybody looking.

'Don't be angry, Cass. I just thought you might have known how we could contact him. I found you in the real estate pages. The funeral's in Otorohanga but not until next Monday. It's going to take a while to round people up. And if we can't find Leo, I guess we'll just have to go on without him.'

Monday. Today was Monday. The funeral was a week away.

'I'm not angry with you,' I said, truthfully. 'Just Rick.' Always Rick.

Then time stopped. And when it started up again it was as though the light had changed. It was as though someone had opened up a black window and pure sunlight now sliced across the floor, in long flat beams, with sharply defined edges. It was like coming up for real air after a deep sea dive where you've been breathing only canned stuff for far too long, Leo's face came back to me, clear and firm this time, and he smiled from the opposite wall as though he'd been thrown there by some new-age slide projector. I could see the boyish smoothness of his skin, the freckles across his nose, that drop of dark hair that would never stay where it was put, no matter how much lick or spit we'd used. I heard him say, that last day, 'Cut, lick and spit, Mum, make a promise.'

He's not ten, I told myself, he's a grown man. And you can't go back because it's not allowed, because neither you nor your body could take it, because going there once was all you could stand. I heard my mother Jenny's faraway voice saying, 'I know, darling, I know. Crying is like giving your heart a wash, but you have to stop it now or it will kill you.'

That had been fine by me. I'd wanted to die.

Even in the laundry, Jenny caressed my face. 'You can't turn the clock back, Cassandra, because the hands won't go. It's like looking up at a mighty oak and baying for the acorn back.'

As Jenny's voice faded, so did Leo's face. I watched his countenance drift off the wall where it settled on the floor as a small hill of dust. That wasn't Leo, that was just my memory of him. I tried to replace him, all grown up, but I couldn't get him right. In the old days I'd pushed him round the neighbourhood so people could say those dumb, sweet things: 'He looks just like his mother'. But Leo would be thirty now, the way I was forty-five. I had no idea of him.

And then suddenly, I was grateful to Rick for at last doing something decent for us, like dying. I couldn't go back for the child but I could go forward for the man.

'Thanks for ringing, Beth,' I said and hung up.

Chapter Two

All the way from Auckland to Hamilton, I drove like a woman possessed. From Hamilton, through Cambridge to Rotorua, I drove the same way. I kept my eyes on Highway One, which neatly bisects the east of the North Island from the west, and headed south as fast as I could drive. I stopped in Taupo long enough to grab a sandwich, have a pee.

I knew if I was a sea bird, a sudden turn west would take me over the land to Otorohanga, out to Pirongia, through to Marakopa where Leo had first seen the sea. I had no wish to go there ever again. I kept on driving down towards Wellington and Palliser Bay.

I remembered how Jenny and I had taken Leo for his first taste of the ocean when he was barely able to walk. As with everything put before him, he'd deemed it friendly and embraced it. He'd put his arms out and raced towards the waves, and we'd had to run to scoop him up before they did. We'd taken him home much earlier than planned, struggling to get a reluctant child into the car. But Jenny and I had been worn out from all the energy spent to keep him safe.

I drove along the Desert Road, the land on either side like flat, tussocky sand dunes, my foot hard down on the throttle.

I flew through Masterton, Greytown and the rest, kept awake by memories and fear.

What would it be like to see him again? How tall would he have grown? Would he be big-boned like his father, or small like me? Would his hair still be the same, unruly, hard to keep? Would I know him if I found him? Would he know me?

Would he be overcome with disappointment to see how much I'd changed? Would he say I'd got old, got thin, got grey? When would be a good time to I tell him what had happened to my hair?

I looked at myself in the rear-vision mirror and ran my hands over the stubble. It had fallen out during chemo and taken months to grow back. But by then, I'd felt very changed. I had grieved over the loss, but only until the hair began to show once again and then I'd taken the scissors to it and chopped the new growth off.

Now, I kept my hair short, like a flag I flew to prove there was no going back. It was a symbol of my victory, of life over death, something tangible to remind me that not all details were important. Hair was not a requirement for good health. And besides, I liked my boyish look.

I kept on driving. After Martinborough there was little else, but I was in the Wairarapa. I was almost there.

When I got to the turn-off to Palliser Bay, I'd been in the car nine hours straight. I remembered little of what I'd seen, mainly just those big square pubs and little country churches that sat on every corner of every small town, shouting location, location, location.

I thought of the kids I'd left behind. My invalid answers to their questions.

'Where are you going?'

'I'm not sure.'

'How long will you be gone?'

'I don't know that, either.'

'Does Dad know?'

'Not yet.'

'You going to tell him?'

Probably. 'Yes, I'll ring him when I get there.'

'When you get where?'

Back to square one.

When I'd checked the fridge for food, there was plenty. No one at home would starve. I'd handed out the lunch money and doubled it for once, before anyone complained.

I doubted Charity would spend hers on food anyway, she'd tuck it away for after school, to spend on better things. Possibly Ty would too. They had different agendas.

Sometimes these kids seemed more Grant's than mine. Yesterday Ty had taken his clothing allowance and spent it on a single gold chain, which dangled against his collarbone and shone up his adolescent skin. I didn't like it. It seemed flashy and indiscreet. I thought it made him appear to be some arrogant Hollywood brat, half-grown and lazy.

But Grant had not seemed to mind. 'It is not as if we are short of money, Cassie. Where is the harm?'

I knew what he was saying, that Ty was simply following the code. To be successful in Auckland, you had to act successful. You spent money to earn it. You wasted it in order to get more. Grant earned a good income and so did I – I'd just made tenth on the national chart of real estate sales – but lately I'd been fighting Grant over his elaborate ways of spending it.

He'd put in a swimming pool, bought us both new cars, matching red BMWs which I thought was ridiculous. Who in God's name needed matching red cars? He'd bought a boat with wide red stripes, which now hunkered in our driveway and had been in the water exactly twice. It didn't mean anything to me, just an obstacle to manoeuvre around when driving in or driving out, but to Grant and the kids it meant a great deal. It meant we were on the right track – the fast one.

And Grant could be the most meticulous man, with his short, efficient sentences, and sweet along with it, so in the end his spending had seemed forgivable. Yet, really, I knew I'd begun to see everything differently from the day we'd bought the house. It was then I'd started dividing things into categories, Frivolous and Required, watching the first list grow to what I felt was a disproportionate length. I'd put the house on that list, right at the top. We'd had a proper house once, with proper walls, doors and windows, a wide and luscious backdrop of native bush. But Grant had swapped it all for a sweeping harbour view. He had wanted this new house, I believed, as a cabinet to display us all in.

'Look, Cassie. The kids will love it. And it is closer to work and school.'

There was glass on four sides, sun but no warmth. The building was huge, with no heart. It seemed to me that half the time Grant and I lived on one floor and the kids on another, and we went for long stretches without ever being together. There'd be a quick hello or goodbye in the foyer as someone passed quickly through, in a hurry to enjoy their own echoing space, but we no longer lived under the same roof.

Our house was big, white and soulless. It had sucked our sense of family up and spat it from the balcony upstairs. We'd had to change our clothes to match. Sometimes I felt invisible. I thought all of us had lost.

But Grant had ruffled my hair and called me a small town Otorohanga girl, except that it hadn't even been Otorohanga but Pirongia, even further out the back of beyond. I knew I'd been as unsophisticated as a doe-eyed jersey cow when he'd first met me, but who was he to talk? His background was not so different. Grant had spent his childhood in Te Kuiti. And besides, I had never been ashamed of my humble beginnings.

The only difference between us, I thought, was that Grant was trying to outrun his origins while I was actively fighting to keep mine. Though making money meant Grant could wallow in some self-indulgent feel-good emotion, to me success was a hollow Easter egg – not exactly satisfying.

Grant worked hard, I worked hard, we had very beautiful kids. That should have been enough. But I knew ambition – a woman's ambition at least – often comes as a wrapper for something else.

As Ty stood beside Charity in the kitchen, he gave me a fleeting glance before picking at the chain he wore and fingering the links.

'Don't worry. We can look after ourselves.'

'Well, here's your perfect chance,' I told them both together. 'No parties, no alcohol, no drugs. No shopping sprees. Got it? Take turns to do the dinner and clean up afterwards. Don't leave it all to Margaret, just because she's there. Just because she's available doesn't mean she's paid enough to be your serf. Don't even think about bunking school because I'll have my spies out, right? And I'll talk with your teachers the very minute I come home.'

'Which is when?' Charity repeated. Her face had taken on a soft, angelic look but I was not fooled. Charity tried on new expressions like little cotton socks. She was too thin, too pretty, and clever enough for both of us. She tapped her foot, impatient.

I had a single weapon but it worked well.

'Any drama out of either of you and I'll withhold your pocket money.' It was hardly pocket money, more bag money, barrow money, their father was so generous with them. But money bought status and power, and these kids liked both.

'And no borrowing your father's credit card, even if he gives it to you on a silver salver, okay?'

'Gold,' Ty said. 'It's a gold card, Cass.'

Cass. He said my name with such disdain, it hurt. I suddenly wondered when they'd stopped calling me Mum and whether they'd ever start again.

'Don't do anything crazy, guys, please.' I hated that pleading note in my voice.

'Yes, Führer,' Charity said.

I'd hoped she been making a joke, but with Charity it was hard to tell. She often said exactly what you wanted to hear, whether it was the truth or not. She could just as easily have said, 'I wouldn't dream of it, Mother', and not meant a word of that either. If I served her up a special dish, as I had a couple of nights ago, she might say, 'Gee, you're so good to me', but it came out sounding contemptuous. My daughter seemed to have developed a total lack of conscience, often cultivating her derisive air, particularly aiming it at me. It was a mystery to me why she did it, but, my God, she did it well.

Ty chose a different route: avoidance tactics. It's hard to remain close to someone who makes a point of not being there. I watched his uniformed back go down the hallway and out the door. He hadn't even said goodbye.

How did it get to be like this?

Both Ty and Charity had been bright, lovely children, but they were changing fast. Last week, while I was dressing for the office party, Charity had come into my bedroom and sat down on my bed. It had been a long time since she'd done that, certainly not since we'd been in this house, and my breath caught in surprise. I knew how much I'd missed her company and that day the blues almost overwhelmed me. She sat quietly on the duvet, adjusted the pillows to form a pen around her, and watched me trying to get the neckline of my favourite dress right, without any cleavage showing. The rim of an awful laceless flesh-coloured bra cup poked over the top.

'Gross, Cass,' she said. 'You'll have to find something else. That's a totally creeped scenario.'

Had I heard her properly? I told myself she wasn't being cruel, just unthinking. Her crime was nothing more than being young. Keeping her distance. Acting superior. And considering my post-op condition, shouldn't her words have really been a 'totally creped scenario'?

But the pain had rushed in, nevertheless. I'd ripped off the dress and pulled on a shapeless matronly top, something that had hung in the closet for years, something I'd never worn.

Now, in the car to Palliser Bay, I felt a different anguish, and this one came from me. It hurt because I loved them. When was the last time I'd said those words to my kids? Did I need to write them on a post-it and stick it to the fridge so I wouldn't forget? I added Grant's name to the bottom. When had I last told Grant that I loved him?

Then I had a sudden, hopeful vision, of putting them all in a room together, slamming shut the door, holding onto their kicking legs and bawling, 'I love you all so much!'

But even in the vision Grant was hard to find, still at work. And Ty retreated at the speed of light to the upstairs lounge, to fling himself onto the sofa and turn the stereo up, while Charity sneaked off to her room to break in yet another pair of shoes. And even in the dream I was left alone, not knowing if my words had soaked far enough into their designer clothes to be absorbed into the skin.

I put my foot down hard and drove to find Leo.

Chapter Three

The road from Martinborough to the sea is not much more than a country lane and the grass grew very green on either side. Black trees rose strong in their paddocks and birds flew from the fenceposts as I rattled along. I smiled at how upset Grant would be with that word rattled. My red BMW would be back in the shop in a flash.

A church, white with a strawberry roof, rested in the middle of a graveyard. When I got to Pirinoa, though if I'd blinked I would have missed it, I decided to take the 'last petrol stop' sign seriously and tanked up.

It was now early evening and my eyes felt gritty and worn, pretty much like the rest of me did. Then I came to a fork in a road and there it was, like fate. On the left, Palliser Bay. Lake Ferry on the right. The choice was mine.

Even the name Palliser Bay produced a deep reaction in me. I stopped, wound down the window and took a great empowering gulp of Wairarapa air. Ngawi, 32 km. Cape Palliser, 37 km. The sign looked new atop its wobbly pole. I chose Lake Ferry and turned right. I knew there was a pub there where I could stay. Even going this way, the wrong way, I felt closer to my past than I'd been in twenty years.

As the car coasted round a gravelled bend, there on one side of the road was a collection of confetti-coloured baches such as only New Zild can produce. And on the other, the wide blue yonder of Lake Onoke lagoon.

Lake Ferry is the name of the settlement, not the lake. When no one wanted a ferry licence to cart folk across the lagoon, the government dangled a liquor licence as a carrot. There was more money to be made selling booze to thirsty patrons than shipping them across the water, and so the ferry ran for years. The old hotel still stands, the last building out on the spit before the road runs into the sea.

I knew a little about the place because I'd searched for it online only minutes after I'd hung up from Beth's call, all the while expecting to see my own sweat and terror dripping on the keyboard. It was a kind of real estate agent's reconnaissance. If I was going to look for property, it would improve my chances considerably to understand the lie of the land. Information had been scarce, but sufficient.

The Lake Ferry Hotel looked like something out of an old novel, long and low and ancient and backed into a cliff of dark green pines. I parked the car out the front on a semi-sealed courtyard, climbed the steps to a pair of paint-flaked double doors. Above, the sky was cream and grey, as though the day was about to end. The wind dragged the clouds around in semi-circles, trying to make room for the night.

The doors were open. Inside, there was no sign marked reception so I banged the small brass bell on the bar. It took a long while before anyone came. While I waited, I stretched my arms, my back, my legs.

'You want to book a room?' The young man's voice was slightly incredulous, the same tone Charity might have used had I dropped her off at a friend's place and asked to meet them. 'You want to come in with me? Why? What for?'

'I know it's late but I've been driving all day.' I picked up a pen from the counter, ready to make my mark. The man's stare made me uncomfortable.

'Don't you want to check the rooms out first?'

'Sure. But I'll take any one of them, regardless.'

I looked around, took a decent whiff of the place. It felt sturdy, strong and safe. The old chipped woodwork and faded wallpaper looked welcoming somehow. It certainly wasn't the Sheraton, but it would do me.

I signed the book Cassandra Johns because it felt the proper thing to do. As I scrawled the long unused surname, I expected Leo to press his face against the windowpane, or show himself to me on the wall, the way he had in the laundry. Leo, still ten, still with freckles across his nose and that funny hair. With the feet that made a skipping sound up and down our old farmhouse hallway.

Instead, I followed a different body down a different hallway, one that ran the full length of the hotel with rooms flanking either side.

'We have six,' the man said. 'A couple with en suites.' En suite sounded remarkably grand, and he knew it. He turned around and smiled. He was tall and, I thought, quite young, though it was difficult to say exactly how old he was. His clothes were nondescript, as dull as the hotel. His hair was a little unkempt, scruffy, but his eyes were full of spirit. 'See? Six rooms. All empty.' And he wandered back down the hallway, flinging shut the doors.

The first room he'd shown me was small and painted lemon, with a pasted flowered trim a foot down from the ceiling and a long unused iron fireplace wearing full-gloss black. There was a large stain on the carpet that could have been caused by wine or blood or both. On the wall over the mantelpiece hung a single painting of the pub itself, a boxed hedge garden running along the front, separating it from the dusty road. In the foreground, Lake Onoke had been daubed on thick and blue.

'This is fine. I'll take it.'

'Great,' he said. 'I like a woman who can make up her mind.' He tossed the key with its knob of beech wood on the bed in approval. 'No meals,' he said, 'well, there are meals but it's a limited menu until the boss comes back with supplies. She's away, but if you're desperate, just ask the cook. That's me and I'm…' he hesitated before smiling again, 'adequate. So how far have you come?'

'All the way from Auckland, today, in one go.'

'Far out,' he said, leaning forward as though to get a better look at the dark rings under my eyes. 'Bet that gave you a fair old time to think about things.'

It was the oddest thing. I felt he had read my mind or something just as crazy. I had done a power of thinking on the drive – enough to last me a hundred years. But then he shrugged as if to say, 'Oh well, so what, everyone's got their stories', turned on his heels and went back down the passage, leaving me alone.

I hooked the mobile phone charger to a power point halfway up the wall beside the bed and lay down with my single suitcase unpacked on the floor. The phone had stayed on all day while I was driving, but no one had bothered to call. I could find easy excuses for Grant. He'd stayed late at work, come home too tired to ring me. He'd turned on the TV to watch the late news and fallen asleep in his chair. No one there to poke him and tell him to get up and go to bed.

He still did that from time to time, slept in his chair. It was a habit he'd acquired while I was working my way through chemo. All those nights he'd said he was reluctant to disturb me.

'I rob you of the blankets,' he'd say, never there to tuck them up around me. 'You need your rest. You sleep better without me. Do not worry. It is not an issue.'

'But I don't mind,' I'd say. 'I'd rather you slept here.'

But even now, he sometimes didn't come to bed. Even now, when I was back selling real estate day after tiresome day, he still sometimes crept in late at night, settled in his chair and stayed there.

'Damn. I did it again, Cassie,' he'd say when I caught him in the morning. 'I must be getting old.'

That was just another kind of excuse.

At the Lake Ferry Hotel, I crawled under the patchwork coverlet and stared up at the damp spots on the ceiling. I could see definite patterns in them. Grant might have been eleven years older than I was, but he'd always worked long hours, thrived on them in fact, never wilting. 'It's us. It's me,' I thought. 'It's our marriage, which, like you up there, is in serious need of tidying up and some fresh new paint.'

It was true. Doing well in the professional stakes did not necessarily mean we were doing so well in private. Yet, I felt a desperate need to ring Grant now, so he could tell me, as he always did, that everything would be all right if we just waited long and patiently enough.

'Have faith,' he'd say. 'It might not happen overnight, but it will happen.' Just like the Pantene ad.

But I was tired, too tired to talk, too tired to argue with his indefatigable logic, which seemed to include everything, these days, except the past. Instead, I lay there, eyes shut, ears open to the weather and the waves. I took a silent personal inventory and tried to see myself as Leo might, if I was lucky enough to find him. I didn't much like what I saw.

The chemo had worked and I'd survived, but much of the life had leached out of me, I knew that for a fact. It wasn't just a matter of tiring more easily than before, or demanding more hours of sleep than were reasonably available – it was more the lack of commitment in the heart and lung department. So few things these days seemed worthy of my energy or my attention.

Though my clients didn't know it, they had been doing deals with the heartless. When I walked them from room to room, I was finding it increasingly difficult to care if the bathroom tiles were home-grown or imported. I'd never cared much about trappings, anyway, and once you've faced your life and death, it seems so very petty to worry over things.

But when it came to selling real estate, I kept the details simple and deals clean. I said, 'Buy this as an investment and it will never let you down.' Investments rarely did. I'd smile as reinforcement – though if the clients had bothered to look closer they would have realised that kind of smile never reached my eyes – and presented with pen and paper, they always signed.

And it was the same with the kids, I knew. When Ty requested a Rolex for his birthday and Charity claimed a hefty cheque just to go to town, there were times when I felt so tired of it all, I'd hardly argued. What was the use when Grant would allow it, anyway.

Somewhere along the line, to save him the trouble, I'd begun to say yes. Yes to everything. Maybe, along with the rest of it, I'd thought who cares anyway?

So that first night at Lake Ferry, when I held up a mirror to myself,

I came face to face with an epiphany. Perhaps it had hunkered down under the rocks, waiting for me to come, eager for its chance to bounce out and change me. Because what I saw was possibly what my family did every day: my own jaded and dislocated profile.

Chapter Four

When I phoned Grant he just said Leo. Leo. Like I'd hauled a forgotten corpse up from a deep blue sea. For a moment I felt guilty, as though I'd spoilt the last of his summer and all subsequent ones to come. Grant repeated the name but still I heard it. Let sleeping dogs lie.

I felt the familiar blunt pressure of old grief.

'Listen, Cassie,' Grant said. 'Do you really want to dig up the past? Do you really want to do this? He is not a boy, he is…'

I interrupted, filled in the space as I usually did, not caring if I was wrong. 'All grown up. Not my baby.' I put these words into Grant's mouth and then I argued with them. 'Isn't that the whole point?' He was mine, in a way Ty and Charity could never be, something I didn't fully understand and couldn't articulate. It had something to do with having him so young – at fifteen and alone. Well, Jenny had been there, of course, but Leo had belonged to me…

The day I'd confessed, whispered I was pregnant, my mother had wrung her hands in horror and held back the tears. She'd held back her sorrow and disappointment too. My plump shoulders had fallen into her sharp bony squeeze and her grip was hard and strong.

'Well, you'll both grow up together, I imagine, you and the baby,' she said.

But later I'd overheard her talking on the phone and understood the depth of her resignation.

'We'll get on with it, I imagine. What else is there to do? She might look all grown up but she's a very young fifteen. I guess what's done is done. No choice but to live with it.'

Now, on the other end of the mobile, Grant copped all the ancient grief as well as the new.

'Don't you understand, Grant? He was stolen from me, like a loaf of bread from the corner dairy.' Easier, I'd trusted Rick. Grant had heard it for so long, I wondered why he'd even listen. 'Which bit don't you get? Sorry.' I lowered my voice. Grant didn't deserve this. He knew the history, had lived through most of it, the only one with enough nous to stay around and pick up the pieces.

'I do not like it, Cassie,' he said gently. 'It is like opening an old wound.'

At the word wound, my hand went into my armpit. When I realised, I took it out and shoved it between my legs.

'You want me to sweep it all under the carpet? I can't, Grant. I'm not going to do that any longer, not even for you.'

Somewhere along the line I'd succeeded in doing what everyone had said I must, to go on, get over it, get a life. I'd swept Leo under our plush carpet and let everyone walk on his skeleton by mistake. But I'd never forgotten. Never. Leo was my son. I finally had a chance to find him and, what's more, I deserved to have him back.

'That was not what I meant,' Grant said, in his formal voice, though his tone was soft and gentle, as though he was sorry too. 'You know that.'

'I'm not coming home without him.' I heard my own voice, thick and strong, reliable, like the one I used to close a contract, clinch a lucrative deal. 'Listen. I'm at The Lake Ferry Hotel. It's not four stars but I like it very much. I'll keep my phone on and with me at all times and you can ring me whenever you want, but I'm not coming home until I've found him.'

Grant's voice got awkward, like a tricky lawyer's. 'Cassie.' He had the habit of making my name sound like the first and last word of a sentence. 'Have you actually stopped to think about this, really think? What will happen if you find him?' He was being very careful but still, he intended to say it. 'What will happen if you don't?'

I felt on the verge of drowning. Grant had turned the fire hose on me, while here I was, just fiddling with the spigot. No, I wouldn't consider that. I hadn't considered that. Not even on my long drive down, propelled along by instincts as strong as my mother's hand in my back. I wouldn't consider it, now. If Grant wanted to be practical then let him, but I wasn't going to be. I knew about practical and I was sick of it.

'I haven't thought past coming here to search for him. I'm here. I'll take it as it comes.'

'How reliable was the source?' There he went again.

'Not very. About as reliable as that rumour about you and Julie Weston at the party.'

I felt his pause and caught the harshness of his breathing.

'Cassie? What are you talking about?'

'Never mind.'

'The source?' Grant asked again, as though he didn't have time for diversions. I didn't have the energy to throw Julie's name back into the rink.

'How reliable? Not. But it's the nearest I've been to Leo since he was ten. And anyway, he needs to know about his father.' I hated that word, father, it was harder to say than Rick.

'What have you told the kids?'

'Nothing. You do it. Tell them anything you like. Make something up.' I knew, for honest Grant, that wasn't a choice, but it didn't matter.

'There is a picture of the accident in the *Herald*.' His tone was neutral. 'The car is a write-off. An old Mitsubishi. They fall apart like a six-pack.'

'Good.'

'It says the sole occupant, Rick Edwards, died at the scene. No mention of wife or children. The funeral is a long way off. Monday.' Then his voice filled with concern. 'You only have a week.'

'Yes, I know. Beth said it would take a while to round the family up. But a week is a week.' Remembering how hard I'd once tried to track Rick down and failed, I wondered if a funeral was possible this side of the next millennium. 'And I guess they're probably hoping someone will find Leo first.'

Someone? I meant me. Perhaps that's why Beth had rung me.

'Do they know you're looking?'

'Not sure.' What difference would it make, I wondered. I'd be here regardless.

'It would take a miracle,' Grant said quietly. 'You know that, Cassie, you do.'

He didn't require an answer. It would take a mother's miracle.

'Do you intend to go to the funeral?' His voice had dropped.

'You must be joking.'

'No, not joking,' he said and his voice softened and fell some more. 'I thought maybe I could hold your shoes while you danced on the grave.'

I enjoyed the picture that made – Grant dangling my high heels from his finger while I did pirouettes on the mound.

'I love you, Grant,' I whispered, not knowing it was going to be said.

'Well,' he sounded surprised. 'Try to take care.'

Chapter Five

I slept twelve hours, which was hardly surprising, since I'd driven 700 kilometres. And when I awoke, I was still so tired I didn't want to open my eyes. I wanted to keep the dream sequence playing in my head. This dream came to me often, as bright and clear as a button and I knew it off by heart. It was lunchtime in a school yard. Always there were a million kids but none of them was mine. They'd be eating lunch like packs of hounds or dashing round buildings at a great rate of knots. I'd be running behind them, frantic, out of breath. It didn't take an analyst to figure out what that dream meant. I was looking for Leo. Of course, he was never there.

But that Tuesday morning at the Ferry, Leo was there in true blue, living colour. He wore the green checked shirt his grandmother had made for him for his birthday, though right from the beginning she'd said she was too young to be called a grand anything. She'd said, 'Boy, you can call me anything you like that doesn't have that grand word in it.'

So when Leo grew old enough to say her name, he called her Jenny, the same way I did.

In the dream playground, Leo wore jeans, his favourite kind of pants. Jenny had helped me cut them down from an old pair of Levis. The label on the back declared they were still a 36 boot leg, but with her help and skill, they had been custom rebuilt for a ten-year-old kid. Leo's hair was long, in need of a cut, out on the porch on the three-legged stool. We'd do that after school, I thought, reaching out my hand to touch it. I'd use Jenny's best pair of scissors and we'd sweep the hair onto the lawn so the birds could have it for their nests.

'We like birds,' Leo said. We had watched them together, lying on our bellies in the grass, trying to work out which were which.

'What's that one, with the suit on and the shirt?'

'Magpie,' Leo said.

'And the one with the yellow jersey?'

'Yellow hammer. Dumb name. Doesn't sound right. Yellow fluffer would sound better, more like feathers.'

When I finally awoke properly it was to the weather, which poured into the room, bleak and cold. Last night I hadn't drawn the curtains or taken off my clothes, just yanked the patchwork quilt up to my nose and slept like that. Now I slipped under the blankets, grateful for the weight of old woollen blankets, so much like the ones Jenny had kept on our beds. Through the french doors I could see the bushes in the garden being thoroughly whipped about by a mean southerly, straight from the Antarctic. Everything looked woebegone, bent out of shape, unfriendly. A couple of plastic chairs flipped onto the patchy lawn and stayed upside down, legs in the air. I could taste the sea, the salt, carried in through the gaps around the ill-fitting sash windows. I went further down into the bed.

My bones had set with a chill I hoped would disappear. But inside, I felt nothing but elated. I was at least in the same weather as my boy.

I dozed for another hour, and then rose, in search of coffee, pulling on Grant's old sheepskin jacket – the only clever thing I'd thought to bring. There was no one about, not even a radio playing behind a closed door. I wandered into the dining room and then through to the bar.

'Hello?'

The place was as hollow as an old beer can.

'Hello?'

I stopped to check out the photos on the walls – there were dozens of them, all taken locally, along the coast. Men in waterproof macs and drooping battered hats, all dominated by the weather and the waves. There were more shots of dangerous water than there were of gentle seas.

I remembered that long ago day on the beach at Marakopa, the rhyme Jenny had tried to teach Leo on the drive home.

> *Don't you go too near the sea*
> *The sea is sure to get you...*

It had frightened me so much, later that night, under the bedclothes, that I had made Leo promise never to repeat it again.

From inside an old oak frame, the Cape Palliser lighthouse stared down from its ledge of rock. Around the walls hung fisherman with whitebait, crayfish and flounder, dark glistening paua laid out on sacks. I peered into their faces and they peered back. I didn't know them.

Outside, the tide pushed into the lagoon, throwing sea spray into the fresh water. It was far too wide to swim unless you were into the Olympics. The wind howled and blew more sand in under the door. A thin mat lifted like a maiden's petticoat and sighed back down again. It suddenly seemed obvious why the hotel had been built long and lean, up against a cliff. A gale like this might have blown a taller building like a box down onto the beach.

'Hello?' I called again. Nothing but the creaks and groans of a ship. No ghostly sailor answered.

I wandered through the rest of the hotel and found a back door open. The man who had yesterday shown me to my room, sat on the porch in a square of sunshine, out of the way of the wind. Looking upwards towards the cliffs, it seemed an entirely different landscape, calmer, and it was warmer here too.

I sat down beside him on the wide steps as the sun poked through a cloud, took my jacket off and draped it round my shoulders and hoped he wouldn't mind company.

'This is an amazing place,' I said, as I settled on the step.

'It is when you don't have to live here.'

'Where is everyone?'

'Hate to disappoint you, darling, but you and me are it. We don't get many people staying here this time of the year.'

He stole a long look at my car parked in the courtyard, if you could call the gravel and disintegrating concrete a courtyard. It was one big expanse of crazy paving.

'And we don't get many people arriving in one of those.'

I smiled. Yes, my Beemer did look conspicuous, so intensely red. Everything else was dune-coloured, grass-coloured, sea-coloured, sand-coloured – all of it stippled with charcoal grey. Even the pub had weathered to fit, with its dull exterior and crooked orange stripes where rust had bled from the window fittings and run down the walls. It looked like an upturned dinghy thrown up by the last king tide.

'If you're wanting to check out, you can't,' he said. 'There's only me around to take your money. And I don't want it. Well, I do, but I might do a runner. Take a trip around the world.'

'So what is this place, the Hotel California?' I asked. 'You can check in anytime you like but you can never leave?'

'Just about,' he said.

'Do you want to go around the world?'

'Don't know. Maybe,' he said, as he turned his head and looked at me for long enough to make me want to stand up, run off. I thought again, in the daylight, that perhaps he wasn't quite as young as I had initially decided. 'Maybe not,' he grinned, as his eyes met mine. His were blue and rested under thick blond brows, and there was enough stubble on his chin for a couple of days' growth.

'Why? Are you interested?'

'Whatever. It doesn't matter. None of my business. Anyway, I'm not leaving, I'm staying.'

'Well, more fool you, then,' he said, then lapsed into silence.

'I hate it here,' he said at last.

'So why stay?'

'Where else is there to go?' he said. 'Here at least I get a room and all the food I can eat, seeing as I'm the cook.'

I wondered, if food was important, what he did with it. He didn't look as though he ate at all. His bones showed through his clothes, especially the ones on his shoulders. He didn't look as though he'd had a decent feed for a week. I watched as he took a last puff on his cigarette and ground it into a patch of sand at his feet, where it stuck up like a tiny flotsam log. There were dozens more. I decided he must have been the cook for some time.

'I'm looking for someone,' I said, taking long, deep breath. I'd kept Leo to myself for so long, now it felt as though I was about to give part of him away. Talking about him hurt, it always did. 'Someone very important to me.' I expected my words to roll around the ground in agony, down the steps and bounce all the way to the bottom of the lagoon. 'His name's Leo. Leo Johns. I was told he might live around here. Well, somewhere in Palliser Bay. Have you ever heard of a Leo Johns?'

And there it was, the full extent of my facts and my fear. But I'd said his name out loud to a stranger and I'd survived.

'Is he your husband or something? Someone that you love?'

Wow, I thought facetiously, this guy is perceptive. 'Someone I love,' I said. 'But not a husband. A son.'

'Ah,' said the cook as though it suddenly made perfect sense. 'Got a photo in your pocket? People looking for people, in the movies, always carry a picture, sometimes in a locket,' he added, taking the piss.

'No. Not a recent one.'

'Well,' he said. 'Makes it a bit difficult to help you, don't it. Leo Johns. Can't say I know the name, but then hardly anyone uses their real name around here, for various reasons. Browneye. Fishfingers. Boatman Bill…' He ticked them off his fingers.

I thought of how even I had used a different name for the guest register. I looked at the cook sideways but his face had fallen to somewhere between blank and serene. At that moment, he seemed nicely uncomplicated. I decided, for some reason, there was something about him I liked a lot.

'Are you here on duty every day?'

'You make me sound like a traffic cop,' he said. 'Nope. I have Tuesdays off. Not that you'd notice. I'm still here on Tuesdays.'

'Don't you go fishing round the bay?' I thought of all the photos on the walls and wondered if one could have been of him.

'No way. I loathe the stuff,' he said. 'Horrible bloody game. Don't mind the fishermen, though. They're something else. Hey, the name's Matt.' He offered me his hand. Long tapered fingers. No rings.

'Cassandra. Cass.' Two on the wedding finger.

'Very nice to meet you, Cass,' he said, but he didn't immediately let go. In the end I took my hand back and sat my bum on it.

'Cassandra, huh?' he said. 'As in the prophet? The one who could tell the future? The one doomed never to be believed?'

Grant had once used the same line more or less.

'Yep. That's the one. And here you are, Matt. Sitting on the step in the middle of nowhere, like a welcome.'

I wasn't sure he'd get it but he did.

'Why don't we just call you Dick, and just get on with it.' He grinned slowly. 'So, how old is this missing person of yours?'

Now for the hard part. 'He's thirty. But you might as well know. I haven't seen him since he was ten.'

'Far out, Cassandra,' he said, as he stared further into my face. 'You have a son who's thirty, who you haven't seen since he was ten. Who would believe it? Not me. Okay, I'll ask around. See what I can find out. Meanwhile, want some breakfast? Despite not being able to stand the stuff, seafood is my specialty. I do the Famous Ferry Fish and Chips…' He spoke as though everything wore capital letters, then paused for effect.

'Thanks, but no thanks.' I shuddered with genuine disgust at the thought of greasies for breakfast. Food was the last thing on my mind. 'But I seriously appreciate you asking.'

'Oh well,' Matt said. 'You'll keep. Detectives always eat. You get hungry from all your detective work and come back and beg.'

'Not if I can help it,' I said as I stood up.

I took a walk instead of breakfast, leaving Matt on the step with nothing to do but fire up another cigarette. The road to the spit was dusty, worn out, no more than bare dirt and fresh-blown sand. It ran for a way in front of the hotel, but stopped at a load of clay unceremoniously dumped to stop traffic, because, a little further out, the road had washed away. A lonely loo, made from a water tank, stood like a sentry on the sand.

I trekked out to where, just like a plug pulled from a leaky bathtub, Lake Onoke emptied straight into the bay. I gave the wind the responsibility of holding me up, and for a while it felt almost pleasant, an albatross banking before it dived, but in the end it made for slow progress, and I pushed on.

As I made my way towards the open sea, cold salt spray swirled around me. Scotch mist. A sign warned anyone who could read not to swim.

> *Dangerous surf*
> *Strong current*
> *Supervise children at all times*
> *Wave patterns unpredictable*

I watched the waves pounding up the beach, could feel their power as much as see it. Call it superstition if you like, but as they sucked back into the bay I felt, even from this distance, that they might take me too. I heard Jenny's long-lost rhyme.

Don't you go too near the sea...

Leo's voice came spiralling down through the years, as he attempted to learn the words by rote, only to be told to forget them. I bent sideways into the weather, turned and headed back. The wind was now a hurry-up, not a hindrance. It blew me back towards the hotel, where my car stood out like a sore thumb, a bright red blob of blood soaked into a grubby bandage.

Chapter Six

When I asked for a beer, Matt the barman went behind the bar in a dutiful fashion and poured me half a pint. A decadent morning beer. It wasn't even twelve o'clock.

'You hungry yet?' He sounded hopeful, like a child.

'Nope. But soon. Promise.' I sounded like his mother.

'You look like someone who would keep her promise, too,' he told me. 'Like those weather chicks on television. When they say rain, it rains.'

Cut, lick and spit, Mum, make a promise…

I took a long swallow of beer. 'I'm not sure if that's a compliment or not.'

'It's not anything,' he said as he wiped the bar clean of non-existent spills. 'So how come you're still here and not high-tailing it over the hills and into the bay for the Big Search. Aren't you meant to be looking for someone important?'

'I don't know where to start.' I fingered the cold handle. 'Winnie-the-Pooh gave everything capitals,' I said. They were for kids.

He folded the bar towel once, twice, then draped it over the taps. Then he stood up and looked at me. 'So what are you so afraid of?'

That was far too big a question to answer and his voice sounded far too much like Grant's.

'Everything. Nothing. I don't know.'

'What's to be so scared of, Prophet?' But then, when he saw my face was set, he gestured expansively around the room. 'Unless it's the solitude. Far out, this place is boring. Listen, why don't you just pop into the future, have a quick scout round, find out what's going to happen next and come back and tell me.'

'Ha.' It sounded like all good ideas – impossible.

'You should stop frowning like that, Prophet. You look terrible when you frown, like somebody's old mother. You'll end up with wrinkles deep as tractor tyre tracks. And what's with the hair, anyway? I don't believe I've ever met a woman with hair as short as mine.'

He turned to look in the bar mirror, where we appeared side by side.

I said what I always did when asked about it. 'I like the butch look. It makes me look like a woman not to be messed with.'

'Nothing personal, but man, they must have used a lawnmower when they gave you a trim.'

No, I wanted to tell him. They took those blades and ran them over my chest.

'It's the billard ball look,' I said. 'Nicely androgynous.' I liked the word androgynous too. I had one breast less than a woman and one more than a man, so I felt I qualified. I doubted he knew what it meant but he did.

'You don't look entirely sexless to me. You just look like a woman with very short hair.'

I pulled a face at him in the mirror.

'There you go again,' he said, 'frowning. Far out. I wish you'd stop.' Then he stopped trying to be funny. 'What scares you the most, do you think? The finding or the not?'

'I'm not sure. It's the not knowing what to expect, I think. I don't know anything about him. I have this huge gap of,' I stretched out my arms, 'two enormous decades. I have no idea what will happen, if and when I find him, prophet or not.' Fear quivered on the end of my tongue but didn't make it into the words. I chewed it up and swallowed it. I hadn't come all this way to be thought a dickhead and a coward.

'Do you want to talk about it?' Matt, like all good bartenders, said.

'About Leo?'

'Yes. Don't be obtuse. About Leo. Your son.'

'Obtuse? That's a big word.' I didn't need a stranger to tell me Leo was my son. Out of spite, I shook my head.

Matt took my glass, refilled it, gave it back to me across the bar, his eyes continuing to stare into mine. Despite my change of mood, it was refreshing to have someone look at me properly while waiting for me to speak, as if my words truly mattered, and not have their eyes slide, slide away. Charity never looked into my eyes, she picked at her fingernail polish instead, and Ty never stayed in a room long enough to encourage conversation. But there it was again. Another horrible brand-new thought. What did I have to talk about that would make them want to listen?

'You got other kids?'

'Two. Ty and Charity.'

'Nice names.'

'Yep. Nice names.'

'Nice kids?'

I wasn't sure. I shook my head to clear it, leant my elbows on the bar. Perhaps looking for Leo had given me a good excuse to run away from home.

'You okay, Prophet?'

'Sure.' I put my hand into my armpit and held on tight. Took it out again, put it where I could see it. Told it to stay there, don't dare move.

'Look,' he said, at last, his voice sounding fatherly and kind. 'Why don't you make my day and tell me all about it. You know, the big picture, the epic story, the Walt Disney version – I've got the rest of the day to spare. No one here to hear it except him, and he's stuffed.' He pointed to a stag head mounted on a wall. There was nothing for me to do, then, except smile.

The story was too big, too much, too hard to tell. But because he'd asked in such a fashion, I managed to give him a single Reader's Digest chapter. How Beth had phoned on a clear blue day, how all the old anger had come washing back and thrown me against the wall. The joy I'd felt when I finally realised I had some proper information to work with. How I'd jumped in the car and driven down here, fast.

Matt the cook watched me as I spoke, as I stumbled through the details, occasionally cocking his head to one side like one of Jenny's chooks, now and then giving me a small nod to carry on.

'The funeral's Monday,' I finished.

'That's not a lot of time, you know,' Matt said. 'You shouldn't waste it here, not in a crappy bar with me.' Suddenly, he picked up an Export Gold towel from the bar and wiped it across my eyes. I was surprised my eyes were wet, that I'd been crying. I never cried. It should have surprised him too, but of course, he didn't know me.

'Not a lot of time to make contact and take him back,' he said, as though I was an alien from a flying saucer, seeking human life. 'Supposing he wants to go.'

'What do you mean by that?' I asked, instantly alert. 'Supposing he wants to go. Why wouldn't a boy want to go back for his father's funeral?'

'I didn't mean the funeral,' Matt said quietly. 'I meant back.'

The tone of his voice, the genuine concern, unnerved me. I wasn't used to people who didn't play games, who didn't push buttons to get the predicted results. I wasn't sure what he meant – I just knew I didn't like whatever was implied.

'What do you mean? Why wouldn't he want to go back?'

'Far out, Prophet, you can't just rip someone out of their life because it suits you,' he said. 'I imagine you've been dreaming about happy endings for everyone, you included and all that.'

For a second I thought he had somehow been privy to the dream I'd had this morning, but then I knew exactly what he meant. He was right. I had been thinking happy endings, thinking that if I found Leo I would pack him up and take him back to Pirongia, back to the old house, back to where he was still a baby, start all over again, without any of the gaps. I would walk him through the missing years, all the way to Auckland, put him a new bedroom and hang his portrait on the wall.

'I'm so sorry, Prophet.' That sincerity again in his voice undid me. 'I really wish I could help you. May I suggest a great big hug, followed by a wee lie down…'

I smiled in spite of my tears. 'Oh quit. I'm old enough to be your mother.'

'No, possibly you're not. Besides, I already have a mother and she doesn't look in the least like you. I don't fancy her, either, if you want to know the truth.'

And there it was, the agenda. He wasn't so different from my children after all. Yet, deep down, I found myself tentatively grateful for his words, his ludicrous attempt to chat me up. I wanted to say, almost in punishment, 'Tell, me, have you ever been with a woman who has had a breast removed? I'm what is known in certain circles as a one-nipple wonder. My word, it's messy, when they take one away, along with all the muscles down your arm. It fair leaves a girl as puckered as an old horsehair sofa. Not a pretty sight.'

I could have gone into greater detail about how I'd considered reconstruction, but only for a second before deciding I couldn't do it. I'd had cancer and survived. Surgery for simple vanity's sake would be like spitting twice in God's good eye.

But I didn't say any of this because across the bar Matt's eyes had lost their sparkle, as though I'd rejected him without any words, as though the story I'd told him had somehow affected him more than he'd wanted it to. Or perhaps he was merely wondering if his speech had offended me and he didn't know how to take it back.

'It's okay,' I told him. 'I'm not offended. I'm altogether flattered.'

'Good.' Equilibrium regained. 'Seriously, I wish I could help,' he said again, and it was obvious he meant it.

'You can. You can tell me about the people who live around here, tell me what they're like.'

'Why don't you come back in here tonight,' he said, sensibly, 'and you can talk to them yourself.'

'On a Tuesday night? Are you mad?' It was my turn to be the comic. 'I thought country folk saved all their money up for Saturday night?'

'Fish don't run according to the days of the week,' he said, with a snap. 'And you can't lift craypots when it's too rough for the boats to go out.'

And his face had changed again, and he did indeed look like Ty or Charity, as though I'd insulted him by lumping him in with country folk, as though, sadly, he found me lacking after all.

I turned towards the window, stared out to where Lake Onoke filled up with silver fish. The tide had turned. If I didn't get a move on, the day would be done. It had been nice while it lasted, but we came from different planets after all.

'See you, Matt,' I said, quietly, 'thanks for listening and for the drink', and headed back through the dining room, down the silent passage towards my room. I would ring Auckland, much more my domain, where I understood the territory. On the other end of the phone, I listened to my own stage whisper telling myself to get lost. I dialled both the kids' mobiles but they were turned off. They were meant to be a two-way street, those phones.

'Repeat after me. I can ring you and you can ring me. Got the picture?'

'Right, Cass.'

Cass. Only it hadn't worked out that way. Ty used his phone for his own convenience, ringing mates as he stalked round the new releases in video shops. 'Which one do you want?'

Charity picked her way through her messages the way she picked through expensive muesli, choosing only the sweetest, plumpest fruits and grains. My kids turned their phones on as they came out of school, but by then they were making better plans with no thought of me.

'What's the point,' I'd shouted once, 'when I can never get you!'

'What's the point,' Charity had echoed, 'when you only ring when you want something. Otherwise you're busy!'

I rang Grant too, but he was in a meeting and couldn't be disturbed. I lay down on the bed and stared at the fireplace shaped like a tunnel. I felt like crawling through it and out the other side. Alice in Wonderland goes to Palliser Bay. All the fear came back.

In desperation and to get my bearings, I rang Sharlands, where I worked, knowing Sheryl would not be in – she spent less time in the office than I did – and intending only to leave a message. But I just couldn't bring myself to do it. I knew she'd probably ring me back to cheerfully abuse me. 'Cass! Where the fuck are you! Don't you work here any more?'

No Jenny around to neutralise the swear words any more.

And I wouldn't be able to bring myself to say, 'I'm looking for my eldest son, the one you know nothing about. As soon as I get my shit together I'm going to go and get him.'

And then what…

Instead, I put the phone down and, to calm myself, started to count the flowers on the decorative trim. By the time I got to a hundred I began to think that Leo would know instinctively I was coming. By the time I got to a thousand I was certain. Leo was over in Palliser somewhere, waiting for me to go and pluck him like a seal off a rock.

Chapter Seven

I didn't go anywhere. I fell asleep, and when I woke the room had filled with darkness. The moon mocked me soundlessly through the doors. Dragging myself upright, I began to throw stuff out of my bag and onto the floor. Jesus, it was seven o'clock. Too late to go anywhere now, except into the bar, as Matt had suggested, and attempt to interrogate anyone I could find.

I looked at my clothes on the murky carpet. What the hell was I to wear?

Eventually, I stood in my knickers and faced myself in the oval mirror propped dangerously against the dresser. My chest was the only thing properly clothed – one bra and one prosthesis.

I'd packed in such a hurry I'd made some very strange choices. A crisp white shirt, a favourite black pin-striped skirt. If I wore that outfit into the Ferry bar I'd look like the IRD. A pair of truly fashionable pants with zips all over the place. Down here they'd turn me into a biker's moll with a Harley Davidson parked outside.

Everything looked ridiculous, even thrown over a chair. I'd worn Levis to drive in, so I hauled them back on, grabbed a T-shirt I'd brought to sleep in, and threaded Grant's jacket up my arms. It was thick and bulky, and far too big, no one had worn it for years, but I was glad I had it. I could hide away inside. No such thing as sensible footwear, either, just my thin leather boots, half-heeled and fashionably unnoticeable. Except that even I could see where the dollar bills had been sewn in with the stitching. I knew I should do a couple of laps around the car park to lose their shine.

The bar was a different place at night, a different landscape altogether. Loud and full to the picture rail with smoke and rugged men – men who looked as though they'd swum ashore, dried on the beach and got thirsty. Fishermen, deprived of the sea by the lousy weather, were now taking consolation in a glass. There were lines around the counter three or four deep. Men aged fourteen to seventy-five and a couple of girls who might have called you mate.

I made my way to the bay window where earlier I'd seen a couple of ancient armchairs, dropped down in one with springs so worn that my bum landed on the floor. I felt exactly what I was here, a rank outsider – over- or underdressed, I couldn't be sure. For some reason, I felt totally annoyed. This was my pub. It had been yesterday and today. My home, at least for the duration of my stay. How could Matt let all these bottom feeders in? I felt like an extra in some Scottish drama, surrounded by large damp actors speaking daft lines in an impenetrable accent.

A week-old newspaper lay at my feet. I picked it up and feigned interest, pretended I could read. But I couldn't. The print wandered off the page and all around the room.

My eyes found Matt's and I pleaded for a drink.

'Beer?' he mouthed over the strangers' heads.

I shook my own with some vehemence. 'Stop fooling about. Whisky.'

And then he was standing next to me, looking exactly what he was here, my one true friend.

'Can you sit down for a moment?'

'Nope.' But he perched on the arm of the other chair and stretched out long sharp-shinned legs.

'God, Matt. I don't know if I like it here or not.'

'You will,' he said in encouragement.

'About this afternoon. Sorry for the melodrama.'

'No apologies required. I asked, remember? Sorry it made you sad.'

'I don't cry very often, you know.'

'Okay, so now I'm twice as sorry.'

'These men…' I said, changing course under threat of a new

billowing black cloud, 'is it possible one of them could actually be Leo?'

'Possible,' Matt said, 'but not likely. Finding him here would be a fluke and I don't believe in them. I doubt if you do either. Nothing worth waiting for should ever come that easy. But listen, get up, move around. Don't be worried by the way they look. Appearances can be deceptive. Trust me, Prophet, there's no one here who would do you any harm, unless it's that one at the end of the bar. Henry the Eighth. He's in mourning.'

'Who died?'

'Only his last wife,' Matt said with a sombre face. 'He's gone through so many. He's on the lookout for number nine. You'd better watch yourself.'

I glanced over at Henry, and then at Matt who now beamed widely.

'I'm only having you on, Prophet, loosen up. These are all good people, good men. Some of them might even do you some good.'

I thought I detected a certain leer. My hand flew into my armpit.

'Why do you keep doing that?' He leant over and took it out as he realised what he'd said. 'Oh, shit, not that. They'd have to fight me off first. Just tell them you're the barman's and no one will touch you, they're too fond of their beer. I simply meant, you could ask them if they know Leo. If they've come across him in their travels.'

'Okay. I'm no wimp. Thanks. I'll mingle. I'm just not used to men who wear gumboots on the carpet.'

'Don't be so judgemental,' he called over his shoulder on his way back to the bar, 'It's hardly carpet.'

I took the last post past Henry and leaned up against an ochre-coloured wall. I knew it must have been white once, but now it was exactly the same shade as the inside of a smoked fish. I wanted to slide down this wall too, but it wouldn't have seemed decent while the man next door surveyed me, head to foot. I decided he, too, had found me wanting. I had the sudden wish to go stand beside Matt on the other side of the bar.

'Cass,' I said. 'Cass Johns.' How easily that name came out. I held my hand out in the hope he'd shake. The man ignored it and went back to swilling his beer. But a different man, further over, listened and watched and moved. He rubbed his hands together before he lifted up his beer. He, too, looked like a shipwrecked sailor, in his tatty Swanndri and boots, but I knew in comparison, when it came to first appearances, which one of us came off worse. My soft-soled city boots and skimpy hairdo didn't cut any mustard here.

I took a headlong dive and spat it out without any pauses. 'I'm looking for someone, name's Leo Johns, about thirty, might be living around here. Any chance you know him?'

He took a long, hard look at me, picked up my hand and clamped it in one of his, but as he did, he slowly shook his head. My heart rose up and dropped again, like bait on a hook.

'Jans Tobias,' he said. 'I'll ask around. You staying here?' I had barely time to nod, before he spun around on his heels and left, walked right out the door.

'Well, I sure scared him off,' I said to Matt, as he glided past behind the counter, coping well enough to make him sweat.

'Jans? He only has two beers at a time. Can't afford much else. Does his serious drinking at home because it's cheaper. Only comes in for company.'

'Really? Well, he didn't seem to care much for me.'

'There's two kinds of company round here, noisy and silent. Jans prefers to listen rather than talk.'

'You want some help behind there?'

'You know how to work a bar?'

'No. But I'm a rapid learner. And I can talk to some of the others as I serve them.'

Matt lifted the flap and I hurried through it, in time to see Jans going down the steps outside.

'He said he'd ask around,' I said as I began to collect up the dirty beer jugs and drop them into a crate.

'Well, there you go,' Matt said.

'Yes, there I go.'

And my heart right beside me.

In the morning, I showered and put on the same jeans and jacket. Things felt different in these clothes, back to basics. Again I went looking for breakfast.

When it came to guests I was the only one. There were a few jars on the tea wagon in the dining room – coffee, tea and UHT milk, and miracle of miracles, one of malt biscuits. I made coffee and took it through to the back door, where Matt sat as he had the day before, blowing smoke rings into the air. He watched me dunk the biscuits.

'I could possibly make you toast,' he said. 'If there's any bread.'

'Toast would be terrific, but no, don't bother. These are good.' I opened my hand and showed him my stash – half a packet.

The day was shaping up to be clear and perfect. Coins of shimmering sunlight fell onto my feet.

'How are we today, Prophet?'

'I don't know about you, but I'm fine.' And I felt fine, too, with my sword polished and swinging at my side where I expected he could see it.

'So. Today's the day.' I knew it. He'd caught the impressive glint from my blade.

'Yep. Today's the day.' I felt brave, almost courageous.

'You planning on coming back or should I get the maid to clean your room?'

I smiled.

'I'll keep my room. Don't change the sheets – I'll be back, whatever happens.' I changed the subject before my silver sword began to tarnish. 'Do you really do it all around here? Everything?'

'Yup. Well, at least while Laurel's away. She disappeared into Wellington a week ago and hasn't managed to find her way back yet. She's looking for a man, see, only she sets her sights a bit higher than the willing blokes around here, a bit higher than she really should, and so it takes a fair old time for her to hunt one down and net him.'

'Fussy, huh, this boss?'

'Nope. Not that'd you'd notice. She sure knows how to choose them, even in Cuba Mall.'

'When do you expect her back?'

'Your guess is as good as mine. She says, "Boy, hold the fort", and then she disappears. I don't imagine she'll be back in a hurry, not even in the event of earthquake and war.' He sounded oddly different.

'Who does this Laurel think she is, anyway?' I said to cheer him up. 'She sounds like nothing but trouble.'

'She's my mother. Who did you think she was? And she's not exactly trouble, she's…ah, Laurel is Laurel,' he said, stealing a biscuit and biting hard on it, as though making it clear he was not in the mood to discuss his mother further.

Then he was gone, thumping off to the kitchen where I heard the distinct sound of dishes being slammed around. It was none of my business, of course, but something I'd said had touched a nerve. I could stand around, try to work it out the way I did every second day with Ty or Charity, or I could get in my car, pray for guidance and go where I was supposed to go, up and over the hill.

I dug my car out of the sand and drove the couple of kilometres back to the turn-off to Palliser Bay. I sat up straight and stared straight ahead. But the salt had dribbled so thickly on my windscreen during the night that it was impossible to see a thing. Cassandra the prophet was just as blind as she'd been the day before.

Chapter Eight

Palliser Bay was once a whaling station, a slaughterhouse, before it became the realm of different men with smaller prey in mind. And it's easy, once you see the curve of the sea, to picture the long boats cutting through the swell amid cries of 'Whale ahoy!' The road flattens up on top of the first long hill, Whatarangi, and for a while you seem to be a bird, drifting, watching, gliding. Then all at once it drops away, so swiftly that you have to use your brakes. And there it is, Palliser Bay, as far as the eye can see.

It was a new tide, that Wednesday, the sea impossibly clear. Any wind had stayed behind on the Lake Ferry side of the hill. The coastline was littered with rocks big enough to tear the hull from a good-sized ship, and yet the bay stretched out serenely, endless and sickle-shaped. I knew that snow-topped mountains stood less than a hundred kilometres away across the Strait, yet I couldn't see them. They kept their heads hidden in the clouds above the sea.

It was foreign yet familiar. Anyone who's ever read books to a small eager child will understand the landscape. Robert Louis Stevenson's *Treasure Island*, unconquered, beautiful and full of challenge.

The country levelled, climbed again, flattened off as I drove along the Whangaimoana Road. I went east because east is all there was. At Whatarangi, the thin tarseal fell into patches beneath my tyres. I lost the coast for a time as the trail went inwards, but soon the road was back beside it again, wandering next to the deep blue ocean.

'Nearly forty kilometres to the end,' Matt had said. Thirty-seven to be exact. But here the kilometres didn't matter. Time had never been better spent. Rather these roads than those in Auckland. I drove on, looking for an unknown place that might cry Leo!

Some chance. With a population of only a few thousand, some permanent and some weekenders, there was only a smattering of baches here and there. No way of knowing which belonged to which. No obvious signs of human life, not even from the cottages with cars parked outside. There were boats of every description, though, boats everywhere, some pulled up from the high-tide mark, and some still on the water.

I followed the road along the teetering, terraced cliff face, where erosion made a frill on the very edge of the Aorangi Mountains, then out and around Te Humenga Point.

Soon I came to Ngawi, and it was exactly the way the photographs had shown it to be. The car stopped almost by itself on the sea bank above the beach, and there they were, the bulldozers, lined up along the shore, corroded noses in the air beside towering boat cradles, as if waiting patiently for their ships to come back in.

I counted them. Thirty. Was that an omen?

In front, the beach dropped away into a milky sea, while white waves rolled stones the size of tennis balls in and out, in and out.

This had to be the ultimate in commercial fishing, I thought. Up on the hill were a hundred cottages. You wandered straight from your kitchen table to launch your boat. And up in the crow's nest, your wife, kids, grandkids even, kept a steady lookout, ready to dish up dinner the very minute you made it home.

There were cabins on the flat and on the rise. On the hill they hung like bird boxes nailed to a wall, black windows reflecting the sea. And over almost every porch swung fishing nets and floats as big as soundless bells.

So many baches. How dumb I'd been to think I might trip over the correct one, accidentally stumble up the right path to my son. And this was not the first bay or the last. The sea roared with laughter.

Don't, I said. Don't.

I would knock on doors. I did it every day in real estate. I would ask around like a professional tout, not to buy and sell this time, but to regain. I set my shoulders in a straight line and looked from left to right.

Behind the houses, one row back, an old man fixed fish-heads into a line of rusting pots. I stuck my hands in my pockets and went to see him. He was deaf and his shouting nearly launched me from the ledge of hillside I clung to. I wanted to whisper Leo's name in this place, not bellow it out so loudly that the waves could fling it back in my face. In frustration, he pointed to the back of his shed. 'Go knock there.'

The woman who opened the door was stout and wrinkled. 'Find Jacko,' she said, when I explained. 'He keeps petrol around and sooner or later everyone runs out and goes to Jacko. If anyone knows, he should.'

I climbed the next zig in the zag and found Jacko, as easily as that, washing windows.

'Goddam spray,' he complained. 'Have to clean the bleddy things every day to see through them.'

I thought, from a realtor's point of view, what he saw was worth it. A panorama like this up north would have the punters gasping. I stood quietly by and waited for him to lay down his hose.

'You're not local,' he said at last.

'No.' I reached out my hand and he rattled it like a pump. 'My name's Cass. I'm looking for Leo Johns.'

'And who might he be, this Leo?'

There you go, Cass, I thought, answer that one. I shook my head; it would take too long to tell him. 'Someone I've lost and I want to find again. Just a friend,' I said, hoping he'd forgive me. And without further ado, Jacko sent me off to NingNong. 'Go three houses back down the road down there. Find Old Ferguson. Nothing much gets past him. People call him the oracle around here.'

'You don't think Leo might be here in Ngawi?' I looked around. I could picture him easily here.

'Not unless he's invisible,' Jacko said. 'Small place. Like living in a shoebox. Everyone knows everyone's beeswax around here.'

So, off I went, again, back the way I'd come along the road.

Amazingly, I found Ferguson easily from Jacko's directions. I followed tyre tracks from a four-wheel drive, and ended up beside a bright blue house.

But Ferguson was under the weather and had taken to his bed. He seemed not only disinterested but muddled and annoyed at being disturbed. He pointed me next door, and into the porch of a Mrs Mulder, who in turn, sent me to her brother even further down the road. The brother had a friend who rented a cottage to out of towners, but that was years ago and he was dead now anyway.

Round and round a racecourse to catch a little flea... I'd played the game all day.

'But I can tell you where it is,' Mrs Mulder's brother said.

He produced a scrap of paper, drew a map, and offered some free advice.

'Never park on the sand, you'll get stuck. Park on the verge. Go back through Ngawi and out the other side. If you come across a yellow dog, run him over, bloody mongrel. Go right past Black Rocks, Te Kawakawa, till you're almost to the lighthouse out Rocky Point, Cape Palliser proper. You'll see the thing with its head up over the rocks. In the cove before you get there, you'll see a tiny little house, like one a kid would draw, you know, way out on its own, with two windows and a roof. You won't see the door because it's round the back. That's my mate's old place, but his kids own it now. They live in town. Buggers, the lot of them, but that's where I'm thinking you might get lucky.'

It was just as well he'd drawn me a map, I thought, as I held it on the steering wheel, in danger of ending up lost before I got there. It was close to five o'clock. The light was paling. Yet, I found the old green bach he spoke of, standing on its own.

The cottage had been built on sand, against all good religious instruction, and a single power line looped up under the eaves. A narrow single-file walking track had been worn in the dunes that led up past the oxidised green walls. It was hard to believe the sheer amount of drift along one side hadn't toppled the whole place over, reducing it to a pile of kindling wood. The lighthouse peeked over the rocks, just as the map-drawer had said. I parked the car on the verge like a good girl, thinking he'd be pleased to know I'd listened so well, and scuffed through the dry grass.

As I came around the side of the crib, all I was thinking at that moment was here's another dead-end for you Cass, you dead-eyed dick. I hadn't thought of food all day and my stomach protested. Some detective. Matt was right. Even the bad ones had to eat. And just as the cook had predicted, I was hungry, really hungry – it was way past tea-time. Demoralised, too. There was nowhere left to go from here except back to the Ferry, back to square one. Back to fish and chips if I was lucky.

At least there was someone home, not like most of the places I'd passed close to by mistake. A lone male stood filleting fish, stooped over a narrow plank set up at a proper height for the job. On the ground at one end sat a barrel, filling steadily with rainwater that ran directly from a tank on the roof. It made me thirsty. I could hear it trickling into the sand. Even over the sound of the waves.

Blood dripped from one end of the table and made dark circles at the fish filleter's feet. He laid down his knife, casually lifted the hose as though he did it a thousand times a day, washed the surface of the bench, wiping it with the edge of his hand before picking up his knife and setting to work again. They were small fish, and he piled the fillets up like narrow pink fingers. Scales had scattered on the ground like fingernails. I saw that the skin on the man's arms was very brown.

He wore farmer's overalls without a shirt. Unlike his skin, his hair was dull, as though he'd been swimming in the sea for years. Some of it fell forward and he looped it behind an ear. He turned slightly at my approach, and for a heartbeat his eyes met mine before they went back to his fish. Slice, pile, wipe.

I didn't know if my mouth would work. 'Please. Please turn around.'

The man pulled himself up slowly, straightened, began looking down at his hands as though they might tell him what to do. Then he put his knife down carefully, turned away, staring out over the sea.

He might have been a pirate searching for a Spanish galleon, or Man Friday on his desert island, but it was me who hoped for rescue.

I stood like the village idiot, unable to move. All I could do was wish, and pray, and hope.

'Please,' I whispered. 'Please, Leo. If that's your name, please turn around.'

But he ignored me. I felt as eviscerated as the fish. Then I watched his shoulders rise and fall, as he slowly began to rinse his hands, still with his back to me. But I saw him. I saw him with something more than eyes. He stood taller than me by at least ten inches, and he was familiar but changed.

'Are you Leo?' He stood so long with his hands in the water that I felt like screaming Tellmetellmetellme! 'If you are Leo, then I'm your mother. Look at me. I'm your mother.'

My hand went into its accustomed place and I couldn't pull it out.

'Please.'

And then, at last, he turned, and only his mouth moved. 'I heard someone was asking about me. So it was you.'

'Yes, it was me, Cass,' I said, staring into his face. And that was funny too. I suddenly knew why the kids at home called me Cass. It took away my authority and reduced me to a mate, but Leo had never called me Cass, he'd only ever called me Mum.

'I thought it must have been you when Jans told me,' he said. 'Somehow, I just knew.'

And that's when Leo's shoulders shook, and he saved us.

I saw his face, like a jigsaw puzzle all messed up. The frame was there, the edge pieces – those were his eyes, that his mouth, there was Jenny's smooth dark skin – but all the other pieces had been dropped and rearranged.

So often I'd shut my eyes to the minutiae of life; now I want it all, every word, every deed. I want every living second denied me for twenty years. I want every single day to remember that reunion, record the sequence of events. You want details? So do I. But I don't remember anything else until he dragged me from the sand.

Chapter Nine

As if by ESP he seemed to wake alongside me.

'Hi.'

'Hi yourself.'

I couldn't get my bearings. We were sitting on a bench made of driftwood, outside his house, against the wall and the whole world was made of ink.

'What time is it, do you think?'

'I don't know. I don't wear a watch. I think it's the middle of the night.'

'How long have I been away?' I couldn't think of another word for it.

'I don't know,' Leo said again, and his voice was gentle. 'Hours and hours. But I've taken your pulse a hundred times to check that you were breathing.'

Hours and hours? Had I really lost that much time with him? What had robbed me of it this time – relief, terror or nervous exhaustion?

He touched my hand lightly, the way the moon can pat the sea, lighting up a path from shore to horizon. All around, the world seemed very black, very beautiful. The sea washed back and forth in a gentle motion, making a wonderful oosh-oosh sound. I rubbed my eyes to check it was for real. Ran my hands over my head to make sure I was still me and still alive.

I studied Leo's profile in the soft light and I could see who he might be – a strange combination of his father, Jenny and me. He was not exactly handsome, but somehow hale and strong. A good nose and cheekbones, but no freckles any longer. Hair so long he could tie it in a knot. There were dark eyes, and short whiskers like a shadow on his chin, Aragorn from Lord of the Rings, whose face once adorned chocolate wrappers all around the country. The longer I looked, the more like Leo, the boy, he became.

'Come on Mum, let's go fishing.'

Mum. I would have swum Cook Strait.

'Come fishing,' Leo said, picking up a bucket and a couple of lines wrapped around a couple of flat sticks. Not a dream, not a demand, just a gentle request.

So, hungry for anything more I might be allowed, I followed Leo down onto the damp stuff, where he pointed out a ledge of rock, way off in the distance where it poked into the sea like Neptune's finger. All around us in a quickening dawn, seals rolled and stretched in their granite beds, looking as though their bodies had shurnk inside their mossy coats.

'Refugees,' Leo said, as he bent down and flicked limpets into his bucket. 'They don't really belong here. They're the ones the rangers picked up sick, fixed up and let go. They don't migrate because they don't know how. They've forgotten where they came from.'

He sounded as earnest as he had as a child and I had to look at him quickly and then away. My heart broke from the loss of him, all those wasted years. But Palliser Bay looked like a sanctuary this morning in all its tranquillity.

We wandered the shoreline to the slab at the end, the one he'd pointed out. In the half light the sea was intensely aqua, the waves amiable.

Don't you go too near the sea... Today that no longer applied.

There was something even in the lazy bark of the seals that implied a welcome. When they raised their flippers in invitation it was all I could do to stop myself from waving back.

Out on the rock we squatted like Indians, as though Leo was the chief and I was a squaw beside him. I watched as he expertly baited hooks with limpets thumbed from their shells, each with its one grey foot and lime green belly. He tossed them over the side and handed a line to me. The few clouds in the early sky were pink and blue.

As easily as a magician, Leo produced an orange from his pocket and handed it to me. 'Welcome to my favourite place in all the world.'

It was a morning to be thoughtful in, I knew, as I threw peel into the water. My heart filled up with a monstrous hope. I divided the orange, passed him half as the seagulls cried overhead. This would be my favourite place, too. Here. Now. This morning. Not so different from the old days out on Jenny's porch, where Leo and I had lolled in a boat made from an upturned table, arguing over which book to read next. I'm sick of reading about men and oars, I'd teased him. Let's find one about fairies.

'Hey! Was that a bite?'

'You're on the bottom in the seaweed. But don't worry, you'll catch one soon.'

Leo took my line, dislodged it, handed it back. I smiled and he smiled too.

'There are all kinds of fish out here,' Leo said. 'Hapuka, trumpeters – you don't have to be far out. The continental shelf sits just off this coast, and then it drops away all at once and the water gets deep. But what we want now is a nice fat moki. They're abundant along here. You can even catch them after a storm because they feed along the seaweed line.'

For a moment he sounded so familiar, offering this vital information the way he had as a child, that I felt the years falling away, into the sea beside us. But the moment passed and when I looked again, he was all grown up and I was sitting with a man.

'This is my favourite place in all the world,' he said again. For some reason, this time, it made me unaccountably sad.

As the sea washed lightly round the rocks, I thought of Charity. I knew her favourite place – Young Originals in Karangahape Road. She'd meet anyone there, even me, her mother, if I took my chequebook along. And Ty's favourite place? Probably at the gym, where he could prance around half-naked and join his cronies on the treadmill, as they talked of new acquisitions: clothes, cars and girls. Grant? I had no idea. It might have been the cleft between Julie Weston's two perfect breasts for all I knew.

'I'll stay here forever. I won't go back.' Did I say those words out loud? I glanced at Leo. If I had, he hadn't heard them. His face remained pointed towards a sun about to wrench free of land. He'd sat like that on his first day of school, oblivious to everything but his teacher, as though she was about to hand him the key to a secret kingdom.

'You go. I'll be all right,' he'd said as he dismissed me. I'd left him on the mat, not exactly alone, but without me for the very first time. 'I'll be all right, promise. You can go home now, Mum.'

'How often do you come here?'

'Every day, if the tide's right.' And it seemed actually to be that simple, as easy as throwing lines into a bucket and picking bait off rocks. 'And when it's a morning like this, I can't help but feel blessed.'

Me too, I thought. The word for what I feel right now is blessed.

'I've got one,' Leo said, sitting up suddenly, hands tumbling over each other, line falling behind us in a knotty pile. 'Only a banded wrasse,' he said, dropping it back into the water. 'Like the spotties up north, only darker. They always hang around the rocks and the kelp.'

But soon there was a different fish fighting for survival: a moki, and a big one.

'You ever eaten one of these?'

I shook my head. 'And never anything this fresh.'

'I'll cook it for you for breakfast.' He threw me a glance that confused me with its shyness. 'Supposing you'd like to stay.'

'Supposing you'll have me,' I answered, 'then, yes, I'd like to stay.'

I soaked up pure gladness before it evaporated over the hill. I could stay. He would let me. 'Leo,' I began, in an attempt to articulate something. But it was too hard and I couldn't do it. 'Don't worry. Never mind.'

And like a man, he didn't wade in with, 'No, come on, now tell me.'

He picked up the fish that lay flapping at his feet. In one deft stroke he slit its throat, while I stole long coveted looks at his uncut hair, his old man's hands, his merciful way with the knife, all of which seemed natural, out here on the rock.

'All we need for breakfast,' he said, dangling the fish off a bloody forefinger while slick ran down his arm. I thought of the fishermen from the city of sails, out to catch the biggest and the most. Not content until they'd murdered a marlin, which would not be eaten but hung on the wall. 'Let's go home.'

Home.

When we got back to the cottage, it wasn't even eight. Leo lit up a gas ring out the back, in the open, the gulls already swarming overhead. When he passed cooked moki to me on a chipped enamel plate, to eat with my fingers, I was so filled with happiness I almost couldn't chew.

Chapter Ten

The bach had just two rooms, a living room and a bedroom curtained off at one end. There was a kitchenette of sorts, a refrigerator but no stove. The furniture consisted of a single bed behind the curtain, a camp stretcher stored in a corner and an odd assortment of chairs belonging to a table with peeling chrome legs. A lean-to out the back took the fishing and other gear. Perched a dozen paces up the hill was a long-drop loo.

'If you stay you can have my room,' Leo said.

'If I stay, it's your bed. I don't want it.'

'But I want you to have it,' he said. 'I'd be pleased for you to have it.'

'I already have your jersey,' I said. 'That's ample.'

I had begun to wear Leo's jersey as though it was new skin. I would not take it off. I would lie in the dunes in it, walk it over the rocks. I would wear it when I slept so I wouldn't have to look for it when I woke. I knew what that made me, too – some greedy, mucky dog, weeing on her spot. If Leo had said he wanted it back I might have bitten his hand. It was nothing but an old black jumper, knitted by unknown hands, its narrative long forgotten. Leo said I was welcome to it.

Its history didn't matter, only the smell of it – salt, sea, sand and Leo's sweat.

I pushed the stretcher against a wall and sat down as though it would fall apart if I didn't treat it with care.

'No. It's your bed. You keep it. If I sleep here, I can see out the window. This suits me fine. I'm so happy to be here I'd sleep upright on the loo.'

'I don't remember you as being stubborn, but I guess you must have been.'

And that was the closest we got that day to the past.

Because the missing years had disappeared and we were just as Jenny had once predicted, all grown up together. Except of course, we weren't – we were more like kids at a swimming hole, skimming stones on the surface of the water, trying not to let them plunge into the shadows underneath.

'But don't get too used to the view, Mum. The weather will change, you know,' Leo warned. 'Is there anything you need? You don't have anything with you.'

'I don't need anything.' I thought of my fancy clothes, and again rubbed Leo's jersey in appreciation. 'I'm very happy with this.'

'If that's the case and you're not going anywhere, I'll row you round the bay.'

Leo owned a dingy, all of three metres long. I watched as he towed it to the water with no help from me. Down on the beach, the kelp lay like liquorice. 'Like liquorice,' I'd tell Grant on the phone. 'How poetic of you,' he might say, except they wouldn't have been my words.

At high-tide mark, there were small black pebbles that glistened like aniseed balls. Those words weren't mine either.

I admired his muscles as Leo rowed, trying hard not to get me wet as he sank the oars deep and pulled back hard. Callused hands gripped the shafts.

'Aren't you hot?'

'Not a bit.' I felt better dressed in my fisherman's rib than in my Trelise Cooper jacket. I would not take it off.

As we dropped anchor and fished again, we made casual conversation about the bay in ancient times. There would be time later to examine the cuts. Let's, for now, just throw a Band-Aid over them to keep any more bad stuff out.

'There,' Leo said. 'Look.' He pointed to the high rock slabs. 'Nga-ra-o-Kupe, Kupe's sail. And over there, see those lines that crisscross the flat? They're stone walls. This is the only place that Maori fenced their kumara crops. They date back to the twelfth century. See Te Humenga Point? That was a once prehistoric settlement. The ancestors of the people around here are buried right along this coast, which makes it a tapu place, but even visitors seem to treat it with respect.'

Up on the highest range, Leo said, was a huge station, where he sometimes went to help muster sheep. 'I take fish up sometimes to swap for vegetables but I'd do it to ride the horse. The people who own the station are good people.' His voice carried a sad and wistful longing. 'I miss the horses.'

I wondered what kind of life Leo lived, that he had to trade fish for vegetables. Nothing but a semi-shack to live in, a man-powered boat and no vehicle. But it was enough for now, just to lie back, shut my eyes and listen to the sound of his voice.

'Remember how we used to play the Lone Ranger and Tonto?'

Leo smiled. 'It would have been so much better with a horse. One day I'll take you up to the Pinnacles,' he said. 'Putangirua. You'll love them. They're totally weird and out of this world. Big stacks of pancakes carved out by the weather, whole columns of them holding up the sky. You know that big cliff cutting you have to go past, at the end of the first bay, the one with all the erosion? Like that only much more dramatic.'

The way he'd said 'one day' had laid a thousand out in a row.

We cruised around the rocks on the way back, close in, where the water shone like thick bottle glass. By then six small moki and a blue cod lay in the bottom of the boat. We went as close to Leo's favourite rock as we could, so he could point out what he called a mermaid's cave underneath.

'I dive for paua here.'

As we arched into the overhang, one small rebellious wave rose up and threw a whole bucket of seawater into my lap.

'You've been christened by the bay,' Leo said.

And that was how Leo learned of my fight with cancer, because in my state of sheer happiness I forgot. I did not intend to tell him, not now, perhaps not ever. I simply pulled the jersey off over my head. I had in mind to wring it out and put it back on again, but beneath I wore only a T-shirt and that had copped the water too. Wet and tight, it clung completely to my body.

I followed Leo's eyes. One real breast on one side, and prosthesis on the other, which now hung down as loosely as an old man's balls. I knew what I looked like too, a sad lopsided contestant in some bar-room wet t-shirt competition. My first reaction was to cover up, but it was much too late. Leo looked at me. He wanted to know.

I placed two hands beneath my bosom, hoisted it up and did a passable Mae West impression. His eyes never left me.

'Okay, I had the Big C but now I'm cured. Officially, they don't say cured, they say in remission, so I'm in remission. Obviously this one's a fake.' I tugged the prosthesis back into place.

Leo's gaze remained exactly where it was, then it slowly climbed my face. I tried to fill in the missing bits the way I always did. 'Okay, it was difficult. It was…mortifying.' That was honest: it had scared me to death. 'Look, I wear this to look semi-normal, but aside from that, no scars.' Well, that was a definite lie. 'There's damage, yes, but it's not going to kill me. Instead, I'm going to live.' Finally, I stopped being funny. 'I had cancer. Now I don't. I had two breasts. Now I don't. I'm okay. I really am okay.' I said what the barman had at the pub. 'You can trust me.'

'That must have been hard,' Leo said.

'Yeah, it was hard. It was difficult. But here I am.'

He said simply, 'Mum, I'm glad.'

'Yes. Me too.' I pulled my jersey back on, to cover up the wreckage.

He rowed out again, dropped sinkers for the final time and we sat in silence, back to back. But it was half-tide and the sun too high on the mast and the fish had gone to nap.

'Time to call it a day.' Leo started winding in his line. Something arrived on the end of it and dropped into the boat. One lonely kina, sharp and prickly.

'Wow. Catch of the day,' I said.

Leo picked it up between forefinger and thumb, leaned over and pinned it gently against my chest.

'Medal for bravery,' he said.

And all I could think, before those tears fell yet again, was that if I hadn't been wearing his old black jersey it never would have stuck.

Chapter Eleven

We came in off the water. Leo dragged the dinghy as easily as a lilo and stood it back up where it lived. There was a name along one side – Leo's Life Raft.

'There's this girl I know in Ngawi,' Leo said. 'Thinks she has a sense of humour.'

I wanted to ask, 'A girl? What girl?'

You can ask a seventeen-year-old and chances are he'll tell you but you can't ask a thirty-year-old man. So I didn't. I sat quietly down on the plank of driftwood suspended between two old stumps, exactly like the gutting bench only closer to the ground, while Leo took the sides off our fish with quick, easy motions. Seagulls danced on the outhouse roof and squawked for a share of the catch.

'You're not going to go hungry, boys, so stop the racket. I'll introduce you to the smokehouse,' Leo said to me. Up beyond the loo was a small tin shed.

'A non-non-smoking restaurant.' He held up a sliced cod. 'They're even better when they're smoked.'

'How long will it take?'

'To smoke one? Not long. Depends.'

'On what?'

He put his head on one side and gave me the kind of look that's usually reserved for the ignorant or very young. 'On how big it is and how much wood there is to burn, Mum.'

'Oh.'

I watched him make a wry face, as if to say, being dumb was quite okay, and I realised, once again, how long it had been since anyone had called me Mum. Strange, I thought, how clearly you see things once you get away. I'd never let Ty and Charity use my first name again.

'And I was thinking, after the fire is set, we might go and have a bath.'

The hairs on the back of my neck rose up. A boy walked over my grave. At one time I hadn't had a bath for five long years, only showers. It had taken Grant that long to convince me I was being self-denying and stupid, and he'd driven me to a motel room and thrown me in a spa. After that I could use the tub again, and almost manage to stand it. Leo and I had always taken our baths together. Despite what my mother had said was 'courting disaster', it had become a problem only once he was gone, when our bathing ritual became yet another symbol of misery.

My voice trembled. 'A bath?'

'Good as, in the river. In the river. What's the matter?'

'Nothing. Nothing's the matter. Nothing at all.'

I swung my arms, a brave soldier, as I walked side by side with Leo, back in the direction of Ngawi, where the occasional cottage seemed to run out of the scrub or down towards the beach.

'Holiday homes, these ones, mostly,' Leo said. 'People come out from Wellington for weekends only.'

I thought of Cuba Mall where Matt's mother was trolling for men.

'You should see them sometimes,' Leo told me. 'They get it all wrong. They cruise out here in their four-wheel-drives and back them down into the water. They worry about getting their shoes wet at the beach – I've watched them. Or they go diving with so much gear, they have to crawl out of the sea on their hands and knees.'

He laughed and I laughed with him.

That would be Ty, I thought, after he'd done the scuba course last summer, his snorkel and mask chosen to match his rubber suit. And Charity, heading off to sunbathe with as much clutter as she could carry from the shops. I looked at Leo in his throwaway clothes, and he fitted perfectly in the place.

'They don't belong here, but you do.'

'I'm not sure about that. But yes, I like it here.' He started walking faster and I had to run to catch up.

'What do you do for money?'

'Don't need much,' he said. 'I help out on the trawlers when they need an extra hand. Guys go missing sometimes after a night in town and they don't turn up. I go up to the station for mustering or shearing, but I'd do that just to ride old Maestro. He's one big ugly bastard, that animal, but I love him. Makes me feel like a superhero when I sit on him. Sometimes I ride him down off the hills with meat for Tineke and then run him hard back.'

'Who's Tineke?'

'She must be a hundred and one, Tineke, but she's still dangerous. Somehow she always knows I'm coming. She'll be waiting by the door, shaking her honeysuckle stick, telling me I'm late, when I didn't even know I was going to be there till half an hour before. She's always trying to pay me back for what she calls my TLC. She puts in an order for me when anyone's going to town, whatever she thinks I need. I come home and find it melting on my doorstep. Two whole litres of ice cream once. I could have drunk it through a straw.'

'So it's like a barter system?'

'No, it's not any kind of system, it's just the bay. Everyone here tries to help each other out. It's not a bad way to live.'

I walked backwards for a while, dragging my heels and making a pattern in the sand. I wondered how long my Auckland friends would last in territory like this. They'd never get the hang of doing things for free, of giving goods away. What would Grant do in a place where he couldn't count his money? And no McDonalds or Subway? The kids would starve in a week.

The water hole, when we reached it, was not much more than a gouge in the river bed, barely deep enough to be called a trickle, let alone a bath, but the water was lukewarm from travelling down the hills. Long ago I'd met Rick on a river bank, but not like this. The Pirongia River had been full of snags, overhung with willows and old man's beard.

Leo took his clothes off and waded in, just like that.

I stayed on the bank, and studied his healthy curves. He had a nice body clothed, but naked from the back, he was lovely indeed. His bones moved easily beneath his flesh, his shoulders as full and tanned as his arms and neck. There was no real fat on him, but he was not thin like the barman, either. I imagined, from a woman's point of view, he was perfect.

Dipping down into the water, he sank his head and swung his long wet hair over his back and down his spine. 'Throw me in the soap. Then throw my clothes in. I usually wash them here. Saves water.'

I did what he asked, still standing on the bank fully clothed.

Then he turned and teased me. 'Come on in. Why be shy? What's to be ashamed of?'

Again words from the past, the same words I'd used when he was small. Two questions in a row, neither of which I knew how to answer.

Why be shy? What's to be ashamed of?

I dropped my jeans, threw my T-shirt in the water, unhooked my custom-built bra. But I held it to my chest, not for modesty, but because it seemed so cruel not to. It had been so long since it had been exposed to anything brighter than a 60-watt bulb.

Leo bent to soap his toes, a polite gesture, I knew, as I threw my bra up the bank and wallowed down into the liquid, trying to find a rise in the gravel high enough to sit on. I went down, down, down…down into a gentler, kinder place. I'd been awarded a medal, and now I was being baptised.

I went right beneath the surface, emerging just in time to catch the end of Leo's sentence. '…a breast might be more important if you were planning another child.'

I splashed water in his direction.

'No way, Bay,' I told him. 'I'm not planning even a cat.'

We wandered back to the bach, clean and hungry and revived from the stream. Back to the smokehouse still belching smoke through the pipe that served as a chimney, with its stack of kanuka cut from the yellow foothills. We should have felt immensely tired, but instead we were strangely high.

'What's the story, Mum?' Leo asked. 'With the hotel?'

'I told Matt to keep the room for me. There are no other guests, so I'm not taking up any space. But if you're sure it's all right, I'd rather stay here with you.'

'I'm sure. Who's Matt? I thought the Ferry was owned by a woman?'

'It is, but it sounds as though she swans off whenever she gets lonely. Matt's her son. Someone else who's lonely. Keeps trying to fatten me up on fish and chips.'

'Don't blame him. You could do with some meat on your bones.'

'That's just what Jenny used to say about you.'

Chapter Twelve

You want to go forward? Go back! You want to go forward? Go back! A storm had rolled in from somewhere during the night. The wind bellowed this into my ears before I was fully awake and comprehending. You want to go forward? Go back!

I lay on the cot and listened.

I wondered if Leo could hear it too, behind his crooked curtains.

You want to go forward? Go back!

I sat up and looked out the window. The sea had disappeared. Everything was cold and steely-wrapped, as though all the weather gods had descended at once and taken the summer away. I pulled my blankets tight around me and lay down again.

'You awake, Leo?'

No answer.

As a boy he'd slept in my bed, the same way that, as a child, I'd slept in Jenny's. I wished he'd come to me now. Either that, or I wished the pair of us could climb into his grandmother's bed.

'Leo?'

When there was no reply, I closed my eyes and for the first time in ages, I thought deeply about my mother. I wondered what she'd say if she could see us now, reunited, both sleeping under the same roof. I imagined her heart would burst.

Jenny, who had been maniacal about money, who could stretch a leg of mutton till it pinged off the table, who had cut sheets down the middle and sewn them back together to see out another year, would be delighted by the practical way in which Leo lived.

We'd never gone without, not even when I brought an extra mouth into the house, but neither had we any loose money to spend. Leo's austere surroundings and lack of material things would please her far more than my glorious house on the hill.

I rose, but kept the blanket round me and perched on the edge of the bed. Called again, 'Leo?' My voice came from somewhere down a long tunnel with my mother at the end of it. I waddled over and put my head through his curtains.

Leo lay in the foetal position, face to the wall. I waited for him to turn over, greet me, but he didn't move and he didn't say anything. I went in, bent to kiss him, like a mother, lightly on the forehead. But I saw his eyes were wide open and his mouth was pinched shut.

'Leo, what's the matter? Aren't you well?'

'I don't understand you. You let me go and then you wait twenty years to find me. Then you simply show up as though nothing happened and act like everything's okay.'

His words hit me like an icy shower, like a window had suddenly been smashed away, letting the outside in. The temperature plummeted. Yesterday he had been warm and mild. I couldn't quite grasp the change.

'I don't understand how you let me go,' he said. 'You let me go with him. How could you do that?'

You want to go forward? Go back! The wind was howling now.

He said it as though it was actually true, as though there was no room for any argument. He said it again and his voice sounded small, although it carried a hurtful, cutting edge.

'You let me go, and twenty years later you just show up and act as though those years didn't exist.'

'That's not true.'

He'd been hauled off like a small chair in the back of a furniture truck, wrenched like a statue out of Rick's flower beds.

'That's not true. It's not true, Leo.' I said it softly as though he was still a child who would hear better if I didn't shout. 'I did let you go, but it was only meant to be for a week. It was a so-called fishing trip.'

Leo rolled onto his back, not looking at me, but staring at the ceiling.

'You must have agreed. You let him take me away.'

'Let him? Is that what he told you, that I let him?' Beneath the old grey blanket my entire body shook. 'Is that what Rick said? That he could take you?'

Saying Rick's name made me come unstuck. The hatred made me blanch. My head began to spin, and beneath the blanket my fingers locked together as though I might never wrench them apart. The anger was there and mounting, riding in for the kill. Rick was a lying bastard, and I was glad he was dead in a wreck.

'He tricked me. He said you were going to Kawhia for a week, but instead he took you somewhere so far away I couldn't find you.'

Australia, the police had said. Regardless, I'd lain awake for years, too scared to shut my eyes in case I missed the headlights of his truck coming up the road, the whine of the engine.

'Leo, listen. Remember that silly safety booklet you got on at school?' Even as I opened my mouth, I knew it was absurd – he'd only just turned five. But we'd talked about it, later, in the kitchen. 'Remember, you showed it to us when you got home? Jenny was making the bread and you were sitting on the three-legged stool, and I found you some afternoon tea, and you tried to read it out, only you couldn't because you hadn't learnt to read yet, so I read it for you. It said that if a kid got lost, separated from a parent, they were to stay where they were until someone came back and found them. "Someone will come back and find you. Stay where you are." Remember? Remember that? "Someone will come back and find you. Stay where you are." That booklet was all I had to tell me what to do. I expected it to work in reverse. I waited on the porch for you. Even when it was obvious your father had had everything planned for months and didn't intend to bring you back, even after Jenny died, I held onto that house and everything in it until I ran out of hope. I left the key in the old place above the door and a note on the kitchen table. As long as I held onto the house, I held on to some part of you, some hope for your return.'

He said, 'Why should I believe you?'

'Because it's true. It's all true.' It took all my courage to stay in my chair and not fall onto the bed. 'Despite what Rick might have told you, it's the truth.'

I didn't think Leo was going to speak, he made me wait so long. In the end he simply said, 'Dad, Rick, told me he was taking me on an adventure and that you didn't mind. That we could stay away as long as we liked. That Jenny wasn't well, she was going to die and you didn't want me to be there to see it when she did. That it was your idea for him to take me off somewhere, away from it all, and you'd let him know when to bring me back.'

Dad. It was the first time he'd used the word and it cut deep into my skin. My hand flew into my armpit and there it stayed.

'You don't know what you're saying, Leo.' Jenny's voice. Gentle, missy, gentle. 'Jenny was sick. She was dying. But we could have handled it, the three of us together, we were such a team. I would never willingly send you away. Never. How can you not know that?'

I hauled his hands out from under the blanket, to hold, to keep us both together, but he dragged his back and kept them out of sight. I grabbed up a corner of his pillow as if to shake some sense into him, but then I let it go.

'They were half-truths that Rick told you. Half-lies. And I can't prove it because he's gone. If he wasn't already dead, I would kill him.' I ran my hand over my head and down over my mouth. 'God, I'm so sorry, Leo. I didn't mean to tell you like that. He died in a car accident on Monday. That's why I'm here.'

Leo twisted back and faced me. 'Great. Fucking wonderful. You only come looking for me when you've got bad news, a real great reason to find me. Piss off, Cass. Get off my bed. Get out of my house.'

Cass.

'Leo, please, you've got it so wrong. We have to talk about this.'

While I'd slept soundly, without even dreams to disturb me, I realised Leo had lain awake trying to get the picture straight.

Whatever was in the frame was the wrong shape, size and colour, and now it was stealing everything from me.

It wasn't the way I'd wanted to tell him about the death of his father, but there was no way back from it now. I pulled myself onto shaky legs and jerked myself from his bed.

'Leo, whatever you are thinking, you've got it wrong. I looked for you for years and couldn't find you. Then when Aunty Beth phoned Monday to tell me about Rick and to ask if I'd somehow seen you…' I heard that come out of my mouth, Aunty Beth, and I didn't know whether to laugh or cry. 'She'd heard a rumour that you might be living here in the bay. I got straight in the car and drove like a maniac. I only stopped twice, once to pee and once to buy petrol.'

He stayed silent but I could see him chafing at the edges of his lips.

What should I do? Jenny? What should I do? I sent out a silent plea. And then I heard some of my mother's old advice. 'Give the boy some room and he'll talk when he's ready.'

'It's taken me twenty years to find you, and I'm not going to let you go now, no matter what you do, no matter what you say. I'm not going to go away, but I'll leave you for a while to catch your breath.' Uttered in the same flat voice I'd used to make peace in the past. 'I'll sit out there and wait. I won't go away. I'll give you a few minutes, then I'll come back and we'll talk some more.'

I wanted to reach out to him, at least throw more covers on him, make him thaw. That's what I meant to do. But as I pushed the stray hair behind his ear as I'd seen him do so many times, in real life and in dreams, said, 'I love you so much, I never ever stopped, but I couldn't find you. You were lost.' I felt as though we were both slipping like sand through the cracks in the floor. I needed to hold him. I needed to lie beside him, skin to skin, rip a hole inside me and stitch him up inside. So, like a fool, I didn't go outside and wait. Instead I jammed myself down on his bed.

'Leo…' I somehow managed it, my stomach pushed into the small of his back while he continued to face the wall. It didn't matter that there was no response. The warmth from his body was all I needed.

I laid my arms over his arms, ran my hand over his hands with the sharp ridges in the palms, and the hard knuckles . Held him close to me, as close as I could physically get, shoved a hand into his armpit, drowned my face into his hair, smelled that long lost smell of him. I kissed his neck and his ear, whispering his name as though I'd only just recently bestowed it on him. Primal feelings leaked from me, the way my breast milk once had done, at fifteen, thirty years ago. We could go on now, with all this feeling, and put the lies put to rest.

But Leo bucked violently backwards and I was thrown off the bed.

And then there was nothing left to do, nowhere left to go, except down the track, get into my car and lock myself away, windows wound up so no one could hear my weeping. I joined the awful sobbing of the sea. Fat black-bottomed clouds foamed across my horizon. Thirty-four ships had been lost along this coast, Leo had told me yesterday. He'd shown me the anchor from the *Ben Avon*, wrecked in 1903. I wondered how many lives had been wrecked along with them. I wondered where the seals went for shelter in a storm when the overwhelming urge was to run away. I turned the key, swung the car around and tore back along the coast.

Chapter Thirteen

They say that when you die, your life flashes before your eyes. I think when your dreams are shattered, the same thing must happen. I flew back to the Ferry, taking all the one-way bridges without looking, shuddering over the cattle stops at Washpool without caring.

Anger is stronger than fear. Why me, why this, why now? I'd thought this standing topless in a cold sterile office while the doctor examined me yet again, yet again.

'Why don't you just write X marks the spot so you don't lose your place again.'

Those stark white walls had been cold enough to be inside a fridge.

'It's not necessarily a death sentence,' the surgeon said.

'No? Really? When my mother died of it?' Pull the other one, Doc, and I don't mean the proverbial leg.

On a chart above his head were answers to other questions I had no desire to know.

Did you know an ostrich's eye is bigger than his brain?

Did you know that tomato sauce leaves the bottle at 25 miles an hour?

Is a woman still a woman if a man removes her breast?

Is a mother still a mother if a man steals her child?

What else had Rick said to Leo? What other lies had he been told?

Leaving Palliser took forever. I sped all the way to the cliff cutting and played chicken with the edge. Going over the hill took longer.

I raced into the Ferry, looking for Matt, to pour me something to calm me, any kind of hard liquor would be fine or two, or three, or four – and then I might be able to sort this thing out, find some perspective.

I ran through the dining room and into bar, as if he'd be there, waiting for me to order his seafood special. Then I headed out to the back where he had a room built against the bank under the pines. I threw myself up his rickety steps and against his door.

'Matt! Matt! Please, please come and open the bar!' My throat was as dry as the wind outside and as full of sand, and I wished the only other living being I knew on this disappointing part of the planet to pour me Scotch with a dozen sympathy chasers.

'Matt! Matt! For Heaven's sake, it's me, Cass, please come out!'

The door opened, and Matt the cook stood in front of me in his bare white feet, blond hair flattened from the pillow, attempting to rub the sleep from one corner of his mouth. He tried hard to look indifferent, but a small smile gave him away.

'Far out, Prophet. I'm glad to see you. I didn't think you were ever coming back.'

'I've been gone one night,' I said. 'One night!' Then I felt my shoulders fall. Tears would be next. I was not going to cry again. I was not.

'No, really, I missed you. Hey, are you all right?' He bent forward and his eyes when they met mine were kinder than those of all my children.

No, I was not all right. I would never be all right again.

He smiled again, different, bigger. 'I'm sorry, but it's hard not to be happy to find some stray woman banging on my door.'

'For God's sake, Matt. I've had a shattering morning. Can I get a drink? Can you come and make me one?'

He flipped his wrist to see his watch, his forearm as pale as his feet. 'And it's what? Not quite nine in the morning?'

Not quite nine in the morning? How could it be only nine o'clock when I felt so achingly tired?

'I don't care.'

He put a hand onto my head and rubbed that too. 'Any old port in a storm, huh?' The battle was short but I won it. 'Well why not,' he said, as right on cue, somewhere on the pub roof a piece of iron clapped. 'Sounds like a perfect day for a piss-up.'

My knees went soft beneath me. 'I need to sit down. I need someone to talk to. I need you to serve me some alcohol so I can clear my head.'

He considered it all for a moment, then pulled me into a room with a double bed, clothes all over the floor and kicked the door shut behind me. 'Come in. I've got a bottle tucked away in this mess somewhere, and God knows, Prophet, I'd rather serve you here.'

I went to bed with Matt because I wanted to, pure and simple, except of course it was neither of those things. Part of me, the angry part, threw her hands up in despair and cried, 'I don't care! I don't care! I don't care!' But another part, further down, made a desperate, feverish connection. I guess I could dress it up, call it need, call it want, but when the cook put his arms around me all I required then was for them to stay there. He seemed a little lost in his own unspoken madness but I knew there would be no rejection, none at all. Safe haven.

It had been a long time since Grant had made love to me. After the surgery it had become an act to prove that the surgery didn't matter, that losing a part of my body could be insignificant to us both. But there were times I'd felt like screaming as he slid gently into me, holding back. 'This isn't how it used to be. It does matter! It does!' I'd wanted him to cry along with me, howling, healing tears. But as always, he'd been the strong man, staying staunch for us both.

But I knew that losing a breast had sexually reduced me, as surely as losing an arm would have reduced my ability to hug. I had less skin to feel with. A flat piece of land where a hill used to be. That's a stupid metaphor, I know, but it's also very right. Imagine, every morning you look outside, admire the view. Then one day you wake up to find it's all been washed away, not washed, exactly, but chopped, bulldozed with a scalpel. But still, you're so familiar with the way things used to look through your window, you can't bring yourself to go near the glass any more.

For a start, you can't believe that what you're seeing is real and not imagined, or can't be shut out with a curtain. Or that you can't get the old view back again, if you wished hard enough.

Grief is like sitting alone in the dark, never being able to turn a light on. There is always a time of darkness, even during the day.

I often pictured the cancer as a cat, curled up on the bed between us.

But Matt had never known the way I used to be. That day of the storm he wanted me, sight unseen. I knew he would take me as I was and not pine for anything more.

I fell back onto the bed and felt his body rise against me, as though he hadn't been close to a woman for some time. Perhaps he hadn't, I decided, as he kissed me with such forceful, unromantic passion I felt as though I was as much a cure for him as he was for me.

And he wasn't careful with me. I wasn't some piece of silly china that might break in two if he grabbed me or banged me down too hard. He was rough and very thorough, possibly out to prove something too. For a single fleck of time, he stopped long enough in his poundings to trace the outline of my face, before losing himself in my blemishes and my bones. Still, everything in his hard embrace felt so loving and good, I expected myself to dissolve into the sheets. His breathing came loud and fast, like that of an adolescent boy.

'Cassandra,' he said, into my mouth, into my neck, before tracing my silvery scar. I held him until I could barely stand it, then I rolled him over and stared into his face.

'How old are you?'

'Why? Does, it matter?'

'No. It doesn't matter.'

And later that morning, in bed with Matt, I did everything I knew how to do. It was my gift to him, and he knew it, though he didn't know what it was for. But for me it was something that would never be enough to pay him back.

Wandering in some foreign landscape, I heard him call me Cassandra. And when I woke he still held me. He'd thrown a long narrow arm over my ruined side, but by then I'd been convinced. In the presence of a real live woman, a single missing breast really didn't matter, and I fell asleep again.

Chapter Fourteen

I let him cook me breakfast – fish and chips. He parked me at a table, delivered vinegar, tomato sauce, salt, a plate piled high with bread and butter I knew I wouldn't eat. He pushed in and out of the kitchen door like a jaunty saloon cowboy, imparting strange bits of knowledge, as though it was now his job to entertain me until the food arrived.

'There's been a pub on this spot since the eighteen hundreds. The first one was made of pickings off the beach, old planks, driftwood, beachcombing stuff. It had a thatched roof, Ripley, believe it or not.'

'I believe you.'

'It was called the Traveller's Rest.'

'Nice name.' I felt rested. Or too tired to think.

'The Beatles stayed here,' he said, disappearing and reappearing again. 'Tour of '64. They got sick of all the screaming girls in the capital and escaped out to here.'

'I don't believe that,' I said to his retreating back. 'How would you know? You weren't even born.'

'I know because they signed the visitors' book,' he said, coming back into the room, where he plonked a pyramid of chips down in front of me, a limp bit of parsley on top.

I picked the parsley up and put it in my mouth. 'Wow. Trimmings. I'm touched.'

'I can show you proof if you like. They wrote, "Groovy man. The boys from Liverpool, John, George, Paul and…" Who was the other one?'

'Ringo. So which one was your favourite?'

'Now, now, Prophet, don't be smart,' he said.

The clock on the wall read twelve o'clock. Outside, Lake Onoke lay calm and quiet, as though the storm had been a figment of my imagination. Unbelievable, the weather in this place, and exotic too, if it had truly once blown the Beatles in. 'Okay, I believe you. Thousands wouldn't, but for some reason, Matt, I do.'

'Good,' Matt said, as though we were talking about everyday things, or things that really mattered. 'It's very important to me right now that you believe everything I say. Thank you for this morning.'

He took my hands across the table, put a chip in his mouth and spoke around it. He grinned so innocently that his next words jolted me upright.

'Your husband phoned last night. Must have slipped my mind not to tell you. He asked for Cassie McClellan. Took me a minute to work out who he meant. He said for you to ring him. Said he's been trying to get you but you're not answering your phone. I said I'd pass it on.'

Suddenly, I saw my cellphone, lying like a dead crab on the floor at Leo's.

Then Matt stood up and resumed his spiel like an enthusiastic member of the Featherston Tourist Board.

'This is the furthermost pub south in the North Island, and we're the only hotel in the whole wide world that doesn't have a checkout time. Far out, isn't that interesting?'

Fascinating.

'We only charge for the nights, not the days, and sometimes, we don't even charge for them. Prophet, are you listening?'

'Of course I am,' I said, absently, full of worry.

'You can pack your bags and go at midnight if you want to, so long as you've haven't gone to bed, and we won't charge you for the night or the morning.'

That actually made me laugh.

'Right. I have your attention. Your husband said to look after you.'

Like I was a fragile piece of…

'Said to make sure you had the best room. I told him you already had it, I just didn't tell him it was mine.'

I pushed the chips away.

'Eat,' he said. 'Food. You need something after all your exertions.'

Now he was punishing me.

He said, 'What on earth have you been surviving on out at the beach?'

I almost said hope and wishful thinking, but the words would not come out.

'Fish,' I said at last.

Then he sat down beside me.

'So, what are you going to do?'

'About Leo or about Grant? Or you?

'All of the above. You haven't told me yet what happened yesterday.'

I shrugged my shoulders. How effortless it is to answer awkward questions that way. Charity and Ty did it all the time and no wonder, but then I changed my mind and spilled it out.

'Yesterday was perfect, Matt. So perfect. I found him, my son, I found him. I had him for a whole glorious day and he took me fishing…first off the rocks and then out in his boat. He has this little dinghy…' But then I remembered the medal he'd given me, how he'd pushed it onto my chest. That terrifying wistful longing – I bit down hard on it. 'He lives out by the lighthouse. He said to stay if I wanted, so I did, I so wanted to stay. But this morning, like the weather, it all fell apart.'

'Well, the weather's improved,' Matt said. 'But now your husband is looking for you.'

'Seems so.'

'What are you going to do?' he asked again.

'I don't know.'

'Then why don't we just go back to bed, work it out between us, between the sheets.'

It was tempting, all that surging, uncomplicated warmth. A little voice, a greedy voice, told me I might as well be hung for a sheep as for a lamb, that I could even tell myself it was payback for Grant's reported sins, for the fling he might have had with Julie Weston.

'No. Matt. I can't.'

'Bugger. I thought that might be the case,' he said. 'He's not even here and already your husband's come between us.' He squeezed one of my hands inside both of his. 'But I want you to know something. I don't know if you do this sort of thing often…' He paused to choose his words carefully. 'Listen. This morning might have been a casual idea to start with but it turned out quite different, at least for me.'

And then he disappeared into the kitchen.

Chapter Fifteen

I drove back to Leo, the BMW hugging the road as though I was putting it in mortal danger by simply choosing this path. Back over the hill, past the tsunami danger zone sign at the Whangaimoana turn-off, back along the terrifying terraces that man and machines had sliced into the cliff, back through Whatarangi and the house shaped like a boat. Round Te Humenga Point. Past Ngawi, the boats, the bulldozers and the string of floats decorating the fence.

I parked my car in the soft sand and clomped tiredly up to Leo's back door. Expecting the unexpected can wear you out. And as I stepped inside, the unexpected happened. Leo was stoned, drunk and stoned, wrapped in the smell of cannabis and alcohol, as thick as musky road kill. As I came through the open door, he looked at me blankly.

'Howdy,' he said, in a semi-American drawl. As a child he'd always played round with voices.

Mine came out in an angry roar. 'God, Leo, look at you! Jesus! What's the matter with you? You're drunk!' The same maternal rant I'd levelled several times at Ty. Unlike Ty, Leo did not ignore me.

'No I'm not. I'm stoned. Well, wasted more than toasted. Actually, it's a tie.' He stood up, pretending to tip something out of the pockets of his jeans. 'I'd share, except I don't have any because I don't smoke. I don't drink either.' And he kept on grinning at everything, including me.

Underneath the weed, I smelled rum. Perhaps, like me, he'd gone looking for some short-lived peace in a bottle. My anger sagged and waned.

'So, look, now I'm starving. What have you got for me?'

Every afternoon straight from school, those selfsame words.

'I'll make you coffee if you tell me where to find it.'

'Haven't you got something sweet?'

No, I thought. Nothing sweet.

A candle stood between us, burning on a saucer on the floor and now Leo shuffled over towards it in his old vinyl chair. The air that circulated through the old padding almost snuffed the candle out. I turned in slow motion and watched as he passed his fingers slowly through the flame.

'Youch.'

'Please don't do that, Leo.'

Once again, in the scattered light, Leo's features were like Scrabble tiles that didn't quite make a word. I could still see us all in him – Jenny, me, Rick – but tonight, it was mostly Rick.

The words were out before I could stop them. 'You look so much like your father.'

'Do I?'

'Yes. His bone structure, the shape of his face. Well, the Rick I knew when he was younger than you are now.' Much younger.

'Tell me about him. What he was like on the first day you met.'

'Why?'

'Because I'm interested. I'm an interested party,' he said, grandly. 'I want to understand how I came about.'

The candle blinked. It would be easier, perhaps more merciful, to speak of him in this light. I knew I could make that first day come back intact. But it was ridiculous, useless history.

'I'll tell you about the last day I saw him.'

'No,' Leo said. 'I remember the last.'

And he leaned back, eyes shut, head tilted. I imagined, in his drunk and mellowed state, he might fall asleep before he got very far, leaving me awake and full of longing. But I could do us both a favour, talk until the stone wore off. I ignored his last sentence.

'That last night, you were so excited, I had a hard time getting you to bed. Then finally, about ten o'clock, you took yourself down the hall and put yourself to bed. I came down to kiss you…'

'I remember the wallpaper, full of flowers. I remember the way they smelled, or maybe, that was you.'

'They were red, big red overblown roses.'

'Then it was you. You never smelled of roses.'

Jenny's home-made lavender soap.

'Anyway, you kissed me…' Leo said, keeping my place.

'I went back to the kitchen to finish making your sandwiches for the next day.' I hadn't trusted Rick to feed him on the trip. The few times he'd had Leo, he'd turned up unprepared, saying men were men and didn't need any fussing over, but to me that had always seemed so careless.

'Jenny found me an old tin to put your sandwiches in, too old and bent to miss it if it never got returned. Your stuff lay all over the house. You'd been packing for three days.'

'I remember,' Leo said, still with his eyes closed.

Then Rick arrived and carted you and your clutter away.

'I watched you go down the drive, one arm out the window of the truck, your father with his out the other. A matching pair. Your grin was visible from a hundred paces.'

'And you didn't wave,' Leo said. 'Because I asked you not to.'

Cut, lick and spit, Mum. Make a promise. Don't cry till you see I'm gone.

'I didn't wave,' I said, though my voice wavered now and didn't want to work. 'I went back into the house, sat down and helped Jenny make the bread.'

'You didn't help. You only ever watched.'

'Yes. You're right. I only ever watched. When she asked if you were gone, I said yes.' End of story.

But that day, shaping, kneading, pounding, I knew Jenny had worked the dough as though she had hold of Rick's flesh. She had slammed the bread into the coal range, convinced that Rick would let everybody down. 'That boy's been pacing round like a sheep dog in a box, waiting for his father, and he was late. I don't think that man or this holiday is going to do him any good. Just teach him bad habits, if you want my opinion.

'No matter how good a woman is, she'll never be a man.'

There was anger in her voice and a touch of envy, and even though I hadn't wanted her opinion, I didn't blame her for it.

Rick turned up when it suited him, often without warning and despite long unexplained absences, Leo always welcomed him. The only thing Rick seemed to be able to offer was fishing trips to the beach, but that had been enough.

The beach was over an hour away so we didn't get there often, not in our old car with no spare money for long trips and Jenny's hairy driving. I'd never learnt to drive. Rick was the only one not rattled by the distance or the drive. He'd turn up out of the blue and say 'Let's go drag the net', and Leo would drop whatever he was doing and run to get his togs.

'We don't need Rick' Jenny said. 'We don't need that kind of man.'

That was stupid; she sounded as bad as Rick.

'No, but Leo does.' I'd tried to reassure her – 'I'm sure Leo will be okay' – but I knew my voice lacked conviction. I knew, as well as she did, that Rick promised things and failed to deliver. I said yes for Leo's sake, because Leo loved fishing, but I fell out with Jenny over the holiday because she thought I should say no.

But I'd been the only one home the last time Rick had called in unannounced. He'd pulled onto the lawn in the middle of our flying game, as Leo and I came flapping out the house, Leo with a lime green tea-cosy on his head and me wearing Jenny's spare specs. We'd almost banged into his truck. Rick climbed out of the cab with a strange look on his face.

'What the hell do you think you're doing?'

His tone and attitude tipped me back on my heels. Why did he have to sound so nasty? We were playing, that's all.

'We're running from Captain Hook. Leo's Peter Pan and I'm the Lost Boy John.'

I took off Jenny's glasses and folded them into my pocket, as though I'd see Rick's expression more clearly without them. But all

I saw was the rage on his face.

'Jesus fucking mother of Christ. The kid's not two, he's ten.'

I wished Jenny had been there to take his swear words away, but she was out.

Rick was so mad he almost stuttered. 'He needs more than this, this house full of bloody women. I don't think you've got all your tyres on the road. I think you've got that disease that turns grown people into babies. The moon is full of green cheese, right? You been taking some of your mother's crazy pills? I bet he still sleeps in your bed!'

Yes, so what of it?

I took a good long look at Rick, who stood like a soldier now, straight-backed and rigid as the barrel of a gun. Leo stood next to him, bewildered, in his make-do Peter Pan hat. Rick was the crazy one. We were only having fun. And if Leo needed a man around, then he needed more than someone like Rick who swung in and out when it suited him.

But there was something about Rick's words that lingered, prodded and poked, long after he had spun round, slammed into his truck, calling out to Leo he'd be back. And the phone call less than a month later, saying he'd take him for a week. Yes, a week.

It was summer, and I couldn't find a good enough reason to say no. A week in Kawhia, how dangerous could that be? My first concern had been to ask Rick not to cut up the fish alive, but to hit them on the head first, anything, to kill them. Leo had come home last time and anguished over even the bait fish, their slow and painful deaths.

'You are joking,' Rick had said. 'Fish don't feel a thing.'

Now, I spoke gently across the room to Leo. 'Your grandmother didn't want you to go but I said yes.'

Jenny said Rick had got you, more easily than he deserved. She'd said what she usually did. 'We don't need him.' I'd said what I usually did. 'No, but Leo does.'

I didn't have a father and I still wanted one.

'Rick arrived, packed you up, and drove off in the truck. And I didn't cry because I'd promised you not to. I saved that until till you were well out of sight.' And what a long crying time that turned out to be. 'That whole week was spent in limbo waiting for you to return. For Jenny and me you were our center of gravity.'

'What are we going to do with all this bread?' Jenny had asked me that morning. Such a simple day, such a simple question.

'I know. We'll feed it to the chooks,' I told her. 'And turn it into eggs.'

It was quiet enough now to hear Leo breathing across the room. His face had changed, lost ten years, become relaxed, like someone young. His eyes remained closed but not clenched against the past. The urge to keep on talking took me over, sat me down. I pulled up a chair beside him, though in my heart I held him in my lap. I had to keep that aura of peace around him for at least a little while, long enough to help heal us both. I attempted to build a bridge from his chair to mine.

'Would you like to hear about the day you were born?'

'No, not yet,' Leo said. 'I want to hear about the day you met my father.'

So I started even further back, and picked my way forward through the debris.

Chapter Sixteen

They played their music loud, those boys who dragged the main street of Te Awamutu in their cars on a Friday night. The few late Friday nights when Jenny and I had been into town, as much for a change of scenery as for the late-night shopping, we'd see them in their revved-up Holdens and Fords. There were locals, and the boys from Pirongia, Otorohanga and Te Kuiti.

There was only one I knew, Beth Edward's brother, with his thick dark hair worn longer than Jenny said was decent. When he drove past, I wanted to cross the street, away from Jenny, to leave her behind, to stand alone, to make him see me. I'd peer in through his windows, while she looked away. The stereos thumped and did something peculiar to me inside. Bruce Springsteen singing 'The River' full-tilt, with a voice to strain your heart.

I had never been in a car with a boy until the day after school when Beth's brother pulled up on the road between me and the bus stop. Beth, in the front seat, moved over quickly, making room for me.

'Hurry up,' she said. 'Rick says he'll take us for a burn.'

Rick had a flat in Otorohanga now, to go with being six foot two and having a new car. I hesitated only a moment.

'We're going to the swimming hole.'

'You coming?' Rick said, as he swung his gaze on the spot where my school skirt rode above my knees.

'Rick got this Falcon with his hay-making money,' Beth said.

Rick took his eyes from the road again and studied me.

'Fancy a swim in the nud?'

I shook my head. 'No thank you.'

'No thank you.' Rick mimicked my reply, making me sound like some poncy girl from England.

'It's okay,' Beth said. 'Rick was only joking, weren't you, Rick? You don't have to get naked.'

'I will, if she will,' Rick said.

Beth jabbed an elbow in his ribs. 'Creep.'

'You can give me a ride home,' I said, shyness disguised by fake bravado, 'but first, take me round the block.' I had chores to do when I got home. Let Jenny worry.

'Welcome aboard, broad,' said Rick, dropping his foot on the accelerator and leaving skid marks on the road. Fifteen minutes later, when he stopped to let me out, he pointed to where my feet had drawn chalky footprints on his fresh new rubber mat.

'Sorry.'

'So you should be,' he said. 'I'll make you clean it next time with your tongue.'

I didn't see them often, Beth or her brother, but whenever they showed up, Rick would give me a lift, a bit of cheek, hang around long enough to show off, before letting me out at the letterbox. If Rick was the only one in the car, he'd lean out the window and tell me he'd let me in if I kept my feet off his upholstery.

Then one day he turned off his engine two hills from home and said he'd changed his mind: I could do anything I liked on his upholstery, particularly in the back seat with him. The throb from his music filled me with excitement and trepidation, Then with adrenaline and fear. When I let him kiss me, I knew I'd crossed some invisible line. What would Jenny say if she knew I was sneaking around with a boy? She was always telling me to make my own mind up, but this was different. According to the way things went around here, I wouldn't be old enough to date until I was seventeen and finished school – three whole years to go. But sitting next to Rick felt crazy-good – it made me into a movie star, different, older, prettier. I imagined his hands on me. I liked the possessive way they gripped the steering wheel.

The road was long and winding, and Jenny was unable to see the car that occasionally dropped me off, but one Saturday I plucked up enough courage to ask permission to go for a swim. 'A group of us are going down the river at Otorohanga. Rick will give me a ride.'

'Who?'

'Rick Edwards. Beth's brother. She'll be there too.'

Jenny rang up Beth's mother to 'satisfy herself' but in the end said yes. 'You can go. Take a hat. Keep out of the sun. Don't do anything you wouldn't want me to witness.' Jenny always said that or something like it.

That was our first Saturday Special, lying around on the banks of the Otewa Stream, with Beth, her friend Sally Han and a couple of stray boys from town, Rick cranking Springsteen up until we could sing the lyrics without thinking. Eventually, he came to collect me… alone.

'Come on. Today you can show me how much you like me.'

That was in the car. Yes, I liked him. When he took his hand off the wheel and stuck it in my lap, I put mine inside and wriggled my fingers.

Down by the river, he parked beneath a weeping willow tree. 'Come here, little Cassandra Johns, and I'll show you what to do to prove you love me.'

When he kissed me I kissed him back. When he put his hand up under my shirt I didn't care, I left it there. When he said, 'Let's get out of the car and get comfortable', I followed him into the shadows of the trees. I put his hand on my breast and left it there until the heat from it burned. I had breasts now, real breasts, ones that stood up firm and high, like the ones Bob Seagar sang about, like the ones on the glamour girls in the magazines in the back of Rick's car. Lying in my bed at night, I'd often wondered what it would be like to have a boy touch them. I'd be proud.

'Don't,' Jenny said in my ear as though she was there that day and watching. 'Don't you dare, Missy. You're never too old to be taken advantage of, Cassandra. It can happen at any age, even when you reckon you're too darned old and smart.' That was the worst her language got, she never said 'damned' but 'darned.' But it was a mantra she sang a lot, with her voice thickening in the wrong places until she hurriedly smoothed it out. Though she'd never spoken of my father or how I'd come to be born, when she sang that particular tune, I knew it was herself, not me, she was talking about.

'Show some pride in yourself, Missy.' More advice, but served up on a different plate, saved for the indecisive times when I'd wondered whether to wash my hair or what clothes to wear.

'Show some pride in yourself, Missy.'

Down by the Otewa it became a useful phrase. I did have pride in myself. When Rick's hands roamed down my body, I lifted them back up to my breasts.

While Rick played around with me, I played around with a whole new set of feelings. I lost my virginity in the middle of that still afternoon. I think I liked the attention. Afterwards Rick jumped into the water but didn't call me in. I plunged in anyway and kicked around like an ignorant fool, not worried about what I had done. I didn't splash in the water. That was for kids.

'I love you, Rick!' I called, as he started back up the bank, trying to get a foothold in the soft loose clay. 'I love you. So now you know!' The deed was done. I watched his broad brown back glisten in the dappled daylight. I lay perfectly still in the water so I wouldn't miss a word when he turned around and told me, 'I love you, too.'

I might have been a willing girl, but as a prophet, I was useless. I could never see into the future, not enough to do me good. Rick didn't acknowledge the words. He went up to where the car was parked and turned the radio up. Springsteen's 'River' boomed over the water, lines I knew by heart – I thought it the saddest song I'd heard in my life.

I'm good with secrets. I kept my pregnancy from Jenny until it got too big to hide. When she finally noticed, she sighed loudly enough to wake up Mount Pirongia. 'Oh Missy. How could you let this happen? You're just a child. It's not fair. You're just a child.'

And those were the words she used too, when my baby was trying hard to be born, two weeks early on an August afternoon, while pethidine jabs came as regularly and effectively as the chimes from the old town clock. Through a mist of terror and pain I heard her quiet plea to the nurse. 'Help her. Please help her. This isn't fair. She's just a child herself.'

The voice of the nurse cut sharp and deep, as I thrashed around on my narrow bed, flimsy as an ironing board and just as stable and I still recognised the cruelty of it a long time later. 'Keep her still. Hold her legs. She got herself into this, she can get herself out.'

When Leo finally made it into the world, it was my mother who held him first. She perched wearily on the edge of a chair, holding a bowl in her other hand for me to throw up in, still suffering as I was from administered gas and trauma. She crooned to my baby in a sing-song voice, and occasionally looked at me. 'Poor wee thing.' Then back to the baby. 'You're nothing but a little skinned rabbit. What will we call you?' she asked.

'Leo.' I'd known he'd be a boy.

Jenny practised the name, and then tacked on the surname. ' Leo Johns.'

Jenny and I had discussed it earlier, what name to put on the birth certificate.

I'd said, 'I guess it should be his father's.'

'Why?' Jenny had refused to consider it and she'd shot me down in flames. 'Why? What's the point? Do you see him? Is he here?'

He must have known about me. Beth knew. I'd had to drop out of school. My mother's voice had taken on that thin dodgy whine that it did when she skirted around the facts of my birth. I had no details of my father. Perhaps that was why I thought every child, regardless of circumstance, deserved to have one.

But I was too tired that day to argue, and besides, Leo Johns sounded fine and sturdy, a pioneer's name. I put Rick's name in the middle. Leo Edward Johns.

Growing up without a father didn't mean you didn't want one.

Chapter Seventeen

Leo continued to doze, not properly awake, but not properly asleep either. I whispered goodbye in his ear as I stood to leave, said I wouldn't intrude any more at this time. I'd go back to my bed at the Ferry and come back in the morning.

He was somewhere far away where I was not invited.

'Yes, okay, come back in the morning. Come early, and I'll take you to the lighthouse and you can see the view.'

'Promise?'

'Cut, lick and spit.'

Once again I followed the road back, up and down and round and round, another half an hour that had never seemed less wasted. At the hotel, Matt had gone to bed with every bulb in the place burning. Down a well-lit passageway, I found a scribbled message stapled to my door. 'Grant says (and I quote), Will you ring me!'

I realised that, once again, I'd left my cellphone at the bach. I knew I should go and use the phone in the bar but talking with Grant right now would let in another person and I wasn't ready. I'd ring tomorrow. I'd give myself the night to forget how badly I'd betrayed him. Because Grant had been there for me, from the very earliest days, through the thick and thin of everything, and he was still there, now that the thin of me remained. He'd saved me from the start, that first day in the Te Kuiti BNZ, where I'd gone to borrow money against my dead mother's house.

'I heard about your loss,' he said. 'I am so very sorry, Cassandra.'

Was he talking of my mother or my son?

'It's not your fault. You can't be sorry for something you haven't done,' I said, repeating a phrase of Jenny's as if by prompt. Only Rick was responsible. And stupid, stupid me.

'I heard what happened to your Leo, that Edwards took him.' He said Leo's name as though he knew him. In a way I guessed he would. Leo's disappearance would have been discussed over every retail counter. But Grant McClellan's face was filled only with kindness.

'What can I do? How can I help?'

He sounded like the good neighbours people talked of over fences, or the primary teachers who said 'Is there anything you need?'. There was genuine compassion in his eyes, but he shied away when I suddenly cried, 'I want it back! All of it! I want everything I had!'

For every hurt there's a choice that follows – stay or walk away. Grant walked up to the batter's plate. 'Tell me what I can do.'

'I need money to help find him. I want to mortgage the house.'

It should have been indecent, sitting across the desk from him, bargaining with every stick of Jenny's worldly goods, disposing of her assets the day of the funeral, but it didn't – it felt too little and much too late. Rick and Leo had been gone for months. My time taken up with Jenny's lingering death, the pain had not subsided but grown substantially worse. I'd never drawn a breath without Jenny. Leo had never drawn a breath without me. As I stacked those sympathy cards, bile and bitterness overcame me. Fine, fine, fine. But when someone steals your child away, there are no cards for that.

I related the story, yet again, how I'd been to the police almost every day, until a sergeant who'd finally known his job had thrown up his hands and explained that they were hog-tied. Hog-tied. He'd actually used the word. Information supplied by the Edwards family suggested Rick had fled to Australia and there was nothing they could do.

He tried to make a joke. Though it wasn't unusual for fathers to fly across the ditch to avoid their financial liabilities, it wasn't common for them to take their liabilities with them.

'He's not a liability. He's a ten-year-old boy.'

I'd wanted to fill up his sergeant's mouth with his justice and my malice.

But the sergeant patted me on the back. 'I know, sweetheart, I'm sorry, but there's nothing we can do now, except suggest you look for him yourself.'

And immediately banker Grant McClellan offered me the maximum mortgage possible against Jenny's run-down house, or from his own pocket, if it turned out not to be enough. When I saw myself reflected in Grant McClellan's eyes, it wasn't someone I recognised as me. Alone and twenty-five, I'd gone from a healthy someone who cared too much to a hollow someone with pallid cheeks, whose only real wish was to wake up paralysed. I no longer knew my place in the world, but he, Grant McClellan, could somehow see something in me, worthy of his time and attention.

His mouth seemed strong yet gentle, his hand firm yet soft on my arm, and I wished to give it all to him to hold – the burgeoning, empty sorrow – while I fell down on his blue banker's carpet and slept for a thousand years.

He walked me to the door, offering prayers and luck.

'Come back if there is anything more I can do. Or even if there is not, come back, let me know how things go. I want to help. I hope you find your boy.'

Yes, me too, I remember thinking. Yes please. Me too.

In my bed at the Lake Ferry, I couldn't sleep. I hated sleeping alone.

There came a knock at the door. Hard. Persistent.

'Go away, Matt.'

'You don't mean that, Prophet.'

Oh Matt, my lover, my friend, yes, I do.

Waves of sadness washed over me, tumbled me over and over, right before penitence for my sins flooded in.

The next morning, I spent a long time in the shower, trying to wash the traces of infidelity from my skin. I would never go there again, so help me. Dressed, I opened the creaking french doors, reached into the sunshine and sat down in a plastic chair. Around the corner came Matt, as though he'd been spying on me, waiting for me to appear. He carried a broom as if he'd been sweeping the concrete path, but I wasn't fooled. He stopped before me and tapped me on the head with the handle.

'Arise, Sir Feelgood. Far out, Prophet, what's up with you?'

'I couldn't sleep,' I said, wishing he wasn't so welcome. Wishing he wasn't here.

'Well, that's funny,' Matt said. 'You slept through all my pounding at your door.'

'I couldn't let you in.' Change that to present tense. 'I can't let you in.'

'Heard you come back last night. Thought you might like to talk.'

'Yeah, right.' That's what Charity would say. I remembered the gentle curve of Leo's face when I'd left him. 'I'm all talked out.' I changed the subject. 'What's been happening here at the pub?'

'Nothing at all,' Matt said. 'Until that mother of mine shows up, relieves me of my duties, I'm stuck here like a limpet on a rock.'

I pictured the ones Leo and I had used for bait. He sighed and pulled up a chair alongside mine.

'Not that it's any of your business, Prophet,' though he said it kindly, 'but right now, I need a break from this deadening place. I thought I might shut up shop, and you could take me for a ride out to Palliser, to meet your Leo.'

I wasn't ready to share my Leo with anyone yet.

'So how is the prodigal son?'

'I think things might be okay,' I said slowly. We'd made it through quicksand and found some safer ground. 'Yesterday, it was as though some of our old shape came back.'

'Good. Hard to fight it sometimes,' he said scratching his feet with the bristles of the broom. 'Wanting everything perfect straight off. Too much, too soon. Did you get my note? Have you rung your old man yet?'

Then I realised Matt would have heard Grant's careful, quaint, old-fashioned speech. Grant had always spoken like that, without apostrophes, every 'i' dotted and every 't' crossed.

'I keep leaving my phone behind, by mistake.' I gave Matt a

sideways glance. 'Probably it's Freudian.'

'So use the pub phone.'

'It's okay. I'm heading back out to the bach again today. I'll ring Grant from there.'

'Where exactly is this bach? You might not get a signal everywhere over the hill.'

'Almost at the end of the road. Just before the lighthouse. Right on the cape.'

'God, I had no idea you were travelling so far every day. Sure it's not wearing you out?'

His eyes fell to my chest. I knew he was remembering my scar, considering the possible weakness from disease. We had not discussed it at any length, so he was entitled to wonder.

'I'm okay. Seriously. And most days I spend more time in the car trying to get across the Viaduct Basin than I do across Palliser Bay. Besides, this time's more productive, here. Mother finding son.'

'Son finding mother.'

I hadn't thought of it like that.

'If Leo's going back to the funeral, then this is your last day. You'll have to leave tomorrow to make it to Otorohanga on Monday, if you're going back to Dorkland first.'

Then Matt sat in thoughtful silence. 'Flag the funeral. Spend another week here at Club Ferry, get to know us better before you throw Leo to the wolves. I can just see the feeding frenzy.'

More quietly, he added, 'Listen, Prophet, you're the best thing that's happened to me for a long, long time, but that's not why I'm saying this. It seems somehow wrong, to come down here, drag his anchor and lift him from the bay. If he's hiding out here, it's for a reason. He'll have one, same as me.'

I wanted to ask him what his was, and what he thought Leo's might be, but he got busy with his sweeping, again, fussing around my legs with the broom, dropping a lid on heavy conversation.

'Look how dirty your jeans are, Prophet. Don't look like a city girl to me.'

I hadn't noticed. Oh well, I'd change. Tomorrow. Next month.

Next year.

'Keep meaning to tell you how much I like the new way you dress. The down-at-heel look. A vast improvement from the day you arrived. You looked so Parnell.'

'Bay wear,' I said. 'Very limited line.'

He stood his broom up against the wall. 'If you're planning on visiting Leo again soon, I should make you another meal.'

'Only if it's fish and chips.'

'Nothing else on the menu until Laurel comes back, and somehow I don't think that will help you. Or me.'

'Why not?'

But he chose not to answer.

'What was your childhood like?' I asked.

I had always known that childhood shaped your future, which is why I'd worried myself sick about Leo, all those years he was gone. Every spin put on a child by life altered the man he became. If I'd grown up without a masculine influence in my life, Leo had grown up without a feminine. I didn't know about Matt.

As Matt sorted through his memories privately, dodging an answer, a family wandered into view, heading towards the spit. They had all kinds of gear with them – a picnic basket, a large umbrella to keep out the sun. The man was way out in front, the woman struggling to keep up. Bringing up the rear was a young boy, looking cold and forgotten as he leaned into the wind. But still he trudged on, head bent, eyes on the ground.

'I wonder what he's looking for?' I said.

'Whatever it is he won't find it.' Matt shrugged. 'That kid reminds me of me.'

'You were left behind too?'

'In a manner of speaking,' Matt said slowly. 'There's a lot of ways a kid gets left behind.'

Chapter Eighteen

I arrived at the bach just in time to see a small black object heaved into the dunes; it sailed way up into the sky, describing a wide arc, before it dropped down into the sand like a stone. A dishevelled, semi-naked man stood and watched it land in the shadow of the cliff. It took me a moment to work it out. Leo, and my mobile.

'Leo!' I shut my mouth and ran. I'd never find my phone in all that desert.

'Bloody thing wouldn't stop ringing. I bumped it and it started ringing and then it wouldn't shut up.'

'You could have just turned it off!'

Leo scratched his head. He looked messy with sleep and still hung over. There was something almost feral about him, standing in the sunshine with nothing but a towel around his hips.

'Nope. Never trust those things. They take you back and remind you of other, lesser days.'

'You used to have a mobile?' For some reason that surprised me. He laughed, amused at the sight of my bewildered face.

'Not out here. Never out here. In a former life.'

A life I still knew nothing about. 'How's the head?'

'Too soon to know. Jans pours rum like you wouldn't believe and then sends you off with a couple of smokes. We stayed up all night, going over things. Jans would still have been knocking them back at five this morning. But he helped me sort myself out. Gave me the best advice of my life. Forget what happened yesterday and work with what you have today, and today, I have you.'

My heart cracked and mended as he smiled. Blue sky on the

horizon, no threat of rain.

'Last night you did your Daniel Boone trick, remember? Passing your hand through a flame. Today you look like the Wild Man of Borneo.'

'I remember that book.'

Perfect timing. 'Then you'll remember how many times I read it to you. You owe me. Take me to your lighthouse, let me climb your stairs. But put some clothes on first.'

'Are you sure you're up to it?' he said. He disappeared into the cottage and behind the curtain.

Because of the cancer?

I beat my chest on the flat side, cautiously at first, and then as hard as I possibly could. It didn't hurt, it felt spectacular. I pulled myself up to my fullest height and stomped towards him. 'I am woman! Hear me roar!' I was one of those Amazonian women who lopped off a breast in order to better pull back their bow.

Something tweaked his mouth up at the corners. 'I meant on those skinny legs of yours, Mum.'

We took off across the dunes like witless puppies, meeting up with the road at the apex of the bend. Around the corner at the far end of Leo's cove, the Cape Palliser lighthouse watched from its pile of rocks. It was an excellent lighthouse, in working order, wearing proper red and white stripes. It could have come straight from the pages of a *Boy's Own Annual*.

'Two hundred and fifty stairs straight up. I do them every day. Well, every second day.' He grinned. 'Do what I do. Keep telling yourself the view at the top will be worth it.' And he began to steer me up the path. As we neared the bottom of the rocky ledge, I stopped and peered up. The stairs were wooden, going one above the other, up against the sheer rock wall. No resting bays. 'The company will be worth it.'

The going up was easy. Head down, bum up, keep climbing and don't stop. Don't look down. Don't fall.

'How are the legs?' Leo asked.

'Fine,' I lied. 'Lead on.'

I was glad he'd gone before me. I didn't take my eyes off his feet. When they disappeared, I stopped and he stopped too, and waited. Finally, his hand came down and hauled me up the last few steps.

He was right, the view was worth it. I was right, too, the company was easily worth the climb. As I stood hip to hip with Leo, the bay stretched before us, far and wide. I felt like a bird in an eyrie, one who had taken over the nest. The lighthouse stood beside us and loomed overhead, and I walked over to its cool white wall, fingered the lock on a bright red door. It didn't matter that we couldn't go in. I felt as though, quite easily, I'd learnt to fly.

I went back to where Leo stood like a watchman, hands shadowing his eyes, staring over Cook Strait as he must have done so many times. 'No mountains today,' he said. 'Sorry. That's a shame.'

'No it's not.'

His hair flapped and fell forward over his face, and I tucked it behind an ear. I yelled to the people way across in Queen Charlotte Sound. 'You're on the wrong side!'

I leaned into Leo, who said, 'Isn't this the most incredible view you ever saw? People drive out here, turn around and drive back and never see it.'

'Then I feel honoured to be here, and that's the truth.' I slid down to the ground, my feet out straight, like a child's. 'How long have we got up here?'

'Hours. As long as you like,' Leo said, sliding down beside me.

It was a new luxury, having time at my disposal. Usually it was something I had to snatch and grab. Here I could conquer a rock face the way Hillary had conquered Everest, and say I did it because I had time and because it was there.

'We knocked the bastard off.'

'Sure did, Tenzing.'

There was no real wind, just a light sighing from the sea, but enough to tug Leo's hair out from behind his ear.

'How long have you lived here in Palliser?'

'Not long. Six months.'

Only six months? Where had he been before? 'Leo,' I began, 'it's your turn now to fill in the spaces.'

'Yes I know. There are things you want to know.'

'Yes. And you.' As if we were playing a game of cards, Leo said, 'You go first.'

'No, you. It's your deal.'

So with our backs to the lighthouse and our faces to the water, that's what we began to do, gingerly turning the pack over to see which hand was dished out.

Leo began to scratch his life out for me while I could only listen. But his face was no longer sunny but sombre, almost grey.

'From what I remember, we did go to Kawhia,' Leo said. 'Only we didn't stay a week, we stayed three days and then we drove to Auckland to catch a plane. Rick already had me on his passport. Said he'd got your permission to do it and I believed him. At the beginning I believed everything he said.'

I knew how easy it had been for Rick, to add a child to a parent's passport, as an extra line, without a photo. I had understood about the passport before the police had told me. It had taken Rick less than a month to have it done. He'd forged my signature. Easy.

'We went to Sydney,' Leo said. 'I think we went there because people in cities are harder to find but at the time it was just part of the adventure he told me we were on. That he'd planned to take me up crocodile country, to the best fishing spots in the world. A holiday in Oz that most kids weren't lucky enough to have. He said Jenny was sick, maybe dying.'

One day Rick talked about swapping their names around for a joke. Ed and Leo Rickard.

'One day Rick bought a panel van, an old white wreck. But when the bloke gave him the ownership papers, he screwed them up and tossed them out the window. "Why put our names on anything?" I think that's when I knew, but there was nothing I could do about it. He dodged all my questions. Wouldn't let me ring you. At first he made excuses and then he just said no. "No way. Don't you like it here?" He said no to writing letters. He said no to coming home. Made me feel guilty every time I asked. The story about taking me away because you had to look after Jenny finally stopped making sense.'

I tried not to see Leo asking to write and being denied. Asking to phone. Asking to go home. Asking to know the truth. Leo had been used to having people play with him, not fight him. I tried not to cry for his wasted wishes, but it was too late. Tears had already splashed my face and knees. Yet, selfishly, I held onto the knowledge that he'd wanted to come home to me, but even that didn't do much to erase the picture of a boy drenched in pain.

'We drove up the coast and it took us months to get to Cairns. He kept saying the good life would start when we got there. But when we did, we camped on the beach, to keep costs down. He said he still had some of the money he'd made in Waiouru, but it wouldn't last forever. I remember I said, didn't he know that forever was the longest word in the English language? I think you used to tell me that. I said, anyway, couldn't he save money by sending me home. But he always got moody when I talked like that, or went deaf, dumb and blind and didn't listen. I learned what not to say.'

Leo described how they lived, with nothing but a couple of sleeping bags, a wok, cooking up mainly rice and fish. 'We kept heading north until the road ran out, right into crocodile country like he'd said. We made it all the way to Cooktown before the wagon stopped.'

'Cooktown?'

'Right at the tip. If you think of Australia as a dog, Cooktown is the flea on its ear.'

Got it.

'Anyway, he picked up a job on a fishing boat and I went back to school, where the kids gave me hell for being a Kiwi and tried to beat the crap out of me.' He looked at me and gave me a wry smile. 'Don't worry. They didn't always win. We lived with Colleen, who smoked ten packs a day, but she was okay. We used to have quite a good time together when Rick was away. She cooked these amazing feasts and gave me a clip round the ear when I asked for cheese on toast.'

He waited for me to comment. 'That was your favourite.' How could any mother forget?

'He'd be out on the prawn boats for weeks at a time. When he came back we had two choices, watch him get drunk or go fishing.' His voice grew flat. 'Colleen and I lived a balanced life. Usually we did both.'

Chapter Nineteen

At the top of the cliff, at the foot of the lighthouse Leo sketched his picture of small town life with deft and certain strokes. He told of the times he'd played cricket on a grassless pitch with hard-edged blokes off fishing boats, an old fridge lying on its side in the dirt to hold the beer and ice. It had been continually hot and dry – endless weather, he called it – and the only time it changed was during cyclone season when it became hot and wet. How, the rare times a plane arrived in town, the whole school was sent to scare the pigs off the runway. How, at dusk, great colonies of bats would leave the mainland for the mangrove swamps, blotting out the sky until they landed. How they got drunk from fermenting fruit during mango season and fell headlong out of their trees.

He talked of crocodile tracks in the sand and dingo prints and how he searched the bush for tree orchids to tie on Colleen's verandah posts after she'd taken him into the house from the donger where he and Rick had lived.

'Donger?'

'Prefab. Transportable building. Like the offices you see on building sites. She'd shoved one out the back to rent, to make some money. It had air-conditioning. It was okay but I liked living in the house.' He didn't look at me for several minutes, but kept staring across the strait.

'But it was the tree of knowledge I remember most,' Leo said as his voice slipped a gear and he struggled to find the right one.

'Let me tell you about Cooktown. It was exactly like something out of *Indiana Jones*, a kind of modern ghost town where not all the people have left. I thought it was really cool when I got there, exotic like the Ivory Coast of Africa. The Thursday Islanders are the blackest race on earth. Three pubs down the main street and a few shops here and there. Kids went into the bars and fell asleep under the table while their old men downed beers. Some of boozers never bothered going home – they'd crash out in the street in the back of their trucks. At one end of town there was a post office which stood all alone, a little fat Queensland building, white with a steep red roof, and mailboxes nailed to a post.'

He shifted his weight on the concrete, stood up and stretched. Then he began to pace a little. 'There was a phonebox too, and I picked that up a couple of times to ring you, but I never understood why I got only the dial tone when I called our number. I thought what Rick had said must have been true – that Jenny had gone into Greenlane and that you'd moved to be closer to her. I didn't know there was a number you were supposed to dial for New Zealand.' He leaned over the railings and looked at the ocean. 'Sixty-four. I know it now.

'Anyway, right in front of the old post office, grew a tree. The tree of knowledge. It grew right out of the asphalt on the road.'

It was a real tree, he told me, and probably very old, something like the twisted tawa at the back of Jenny's house, with a sturdy trunk too wide for a eleven-year-old to put his arms around and a big green umbrella up above.

He coughed to clear his throat. 'I passed it every day on my way to school. Every day I stopped to read the messages. It was covered in all these notes.'

Then Leo described how pieces of paper would be tacked to the tree as though it was some cheap noticeboard – flyers for houses wanted, houses available, plugs for visiting musicians hopeful of captive audience, quiz nights at the pub, good deals at the grocery store. Boats for sale. Fishing hands wanted. Farm hands required. Horses to be broken in. Kittens to be given away. Dogs missing. Dogs found.

'I used to stand at the bottom, every day, thinking there might be something for me.'

Boy wanted.

'Stupid, isn't it. But something, anything, with my old name on it. Something from home. From you.'

Boy lost.

He attempted to shake it off, like a yoke from round his neck, by moving further along his story, but suddenly it all seemed far too much and far too painful for both of us. I lost the ability to listen, there came such roaring in my ears. His loss had been dreadful, equal to mine, worse. I could see it in his body movements, the hunch of his neck. All the loss I'd been handed, Leo had worn too.

His voice broke through my pain barrier. 'Rick got a job as ranch hand on a station and we left and life changed again. And the only good thing about station life was my dog.'

Slowly, so as not to lose anything, I brought myself back to the here and now. 'Shhh,' I told him, leaning over the railing with him, holding him safe on my side of the rock. 'Shhh. No more now.'

We came down from our eagle perch before dusk hit the water and it was harder coming down than going up. My mind kept making tracks around the Australian countryside, while my legs kept strictly to the stairs. But Leo went down below me, to catch me if I fell. How my heart hurt, not for me, but for my son.

And I still hadn't mentioned the funeral. Leo didn't know he had a sister or brother or that I had a husband called Grant. And there were all those other details, extra to the ones he had supplied. My story. The things I might say that would help him, like how much time I had spent desperately looking for him.

By the time we reached the bottom, my legs were about as steady as a stool made of biscuits. I lay down on my back in the sand. 'My God. How many steps did you say there were? Two and a half thousand?'

Leo squatted beside me. 'If you stay here long enough, you'll get fit.'

I wanted to tell him how much I loved him, how badly I wanted to stay, but for some reason Matt's voice flew in. Too much, too soon, it said. So instead, I said, 'I've been meaning to talk to you about

Rick's funeral. It's Monday, which means, if we're going, we'll have to leave tomorrow, Sunday.'

I watched his head jerk up. 'What are you talking about? You talk as though it's all planned.'

I sat up. 'I know we haven't talked about it, but…' I'd made a gap and now I couldn't find any words to fill it. 'I don't understand your reaction.' Then for a second, I thought I did. 'If it's about money, you don't have to worry. I've got money. It's not like in the old days. We're not broke any more.'

'They can bury him without me,' Leo said.

'But surely…' I groped for the right words. 'He was your father…' Somehow, I expected that would still count.

The edge in his voice was easing but much of it was still there. 'You want to know how long it's been since I saw him last? I was sixteen. You count the years up.'

I knew immediately. The tally was fourteen. And there on the ground, my heart spat its last breath and began to disintegrate. Rick had held onto Leo for six short years. Six short years! What had happened to my baby after that?

'We've had enough of revisiting the past for one day,' Leo said sharply, as though he could read my mind. 'Listen. I think we'll park this up, write X marks the spot, come back to it later. I meant to tell you, there's a party tonight at Jans's place, in Ngawi. It's probably in your honour because he wants to give you a feed of crayfish. I promised him we would go, but if we don't stop talking about this…'

I didn't let him finish. 'Everyone here wants to feed me up,' I said miserably, trying to get my voice to sound normal. I couldn't have cared less about crayfish but I wouldn't embarrass Leo by not turning up, and I wouldn't turn down a chance to meet his friends.

'Okay. You're right. But I warn you, I might need a rest first.' I pointed to my knees.

Leo's laughter rang out again at last. I welcomed the sound of it. 'Ha! Race you!'

But life isn't a tidy thing, it's full of tatty ends. As we rounded the dunes towards the bach, gulls lifted and scattered in our path. One dropped his processed dinner on my head. I was about to ask Leo if a seagull dumping on you in Palliser Bay could be deemed a blessing or a curse, when a car came round the bend in the road, chased by a plume of dust. An identical car to mine pulled up on the leeward side of the grass, red paintwork barely showing through the grime. But even with its Wairarapa coat on, it looked ridiculous and red. The image was like something out of a Saatchi & Saatchi ad.

'Snap,' Leo said.

'No.' I said, 'it's shit.'

Chapter Twenty

I couldn't help it. All the way over the dunes to the bach I felt perversely annoyed with Grant for coming out to find me. But the first words that came into my head when I saw his worn, everyday face, Matt following close behind with a genuinely amused expression, were more of Jenny's and not mine. 'Experience is a hard teacher. She gives the questions first, the lessons after.'

Whatever this test turned out to be, I was sure I'd already failed.

'Cassie,' Grant said, moving towards me across the sand, hands out as if to lift me up, sit me down, hold me tight whether I wanted it or not. When I flinched, he noticed immediately, stepped back and stayed there, his weight on a well-shod foot. Grant might be my husband, but I didn't want to be hugged, not in front of Matt or my son. My loyalties splintered. What I wanted was everything to go back to how it was an hour or so before, back to being just Leo and me.

'Evening, Prophet,' said Matt out of one side of his mouth, as though enjoying this very bad joke.

Leo had stopped somewhere back behind me. I wanted to run back to him, take him away, start the day again – take me to your lighthouse, let me climb your stairs – but now the day was over.

'I left early this morning,' Grant said. 'Before it got light. Matt here said he could find you from what you had said. What is the matter?'

I couldn't explain it. In some strange subversive tactic, I'd left my cellphone in the bach so Grant couldn't keep in touch, until he felt he had to come down to Lake Ferry to see for himself what was what. Even lost in the sand dunes, somehow my phone had summoned my husband down to Palliser Bay where I wasn't ready to see him.

'By the way, Charity and Ty say hi. Charity said to remind you about the ball.'

I repeated sickly, 'The ball?'

'You know. The dress,' Grant said.

Only Charity could send a message that related entirely to herself, and only Grant could be so good as to deliver it to me, in this place. I looked aghast at Leo; he hadn't moved.

'Please, Matt, take Grant back to the pub.'

'Cassie. What is the matter with you?' Grant asked again. I thought he must surely see how fractured my head and body were, feel the heat from ruined leg muscles through my unwashed jeans.

'Actually, I'm not in a hurry to leave, Cassie,' Matt said, deliberately using Grant's name for me. 'Laurel's back, see? The jailer's got the keys.'

Perfect, I thought. Fantastic. And you and Grant have come out here to put me away.

'Look. Why don't we all sit down somewhere,' Grant said, sensibly, looking around as if a boardroom table and chairs might materialise in the sand. But I didn't want him here, or Matt either. They were interlopers, intruders in family rites that were none of their business and nowhere near completed.

'If you could just do something for me, Grant, I'd be grateful. Go away, and I'll explain later.' Out the corner of my eye, I saw Leo making his way down to the rocks on the shore, almost out of sight. I felt distraught. If he disappeared now, I might not get him back and there was no guarantee I'd get a second chance. And if Matt wasn't careful, it could be Grant who disappeared next, off my personal radar screen. 'If you could just go back to the pub, I'll see you there later. I don't know when, but I will come as soon as I can, I promise. Leo and I still have things we have to do.'

I turned to Matt. 'Thanks for bringing him here, I mean it, truly, but if you could just take him back, I'd be grateful to you as well.'

'How grateful?'

I ignored it. I didn't blame him for taunting me. Here I was, surrounded by men who could be considered competitors. 'Please, both of you. Go back to the pub. Have a beer together. I'll see you later on tonight.'

They both stared as though I'd set a date for three months hence.

I grabbed my husband's hand. 'What's happening here is private, Grant, you know that. Leo and I – we've waited so long. I'll come back to the Ferry tonight and I'll bring him with me if he wants to come, and then you can meet him properly.'

Leo was now making his way further over the rocks, heading south, as though he was about to walk into the water and start to swim. I knew where he was going too, out to the sliver of foreshore he'd called his favourite place in the world. Going away from me, without me.

'Please, Grant.'

Matt sat down on his heels to light the inevitable cigarette, while Grant ran a hand through thinning hair. I heard it plainly when he spoke, disappointment edged with care, but there was resignation in there too. 'Okay. We will go. Are you sure that you are all right?'

'Yes. I'm all right.' I squeezed his hand, and stepped up and let him kiss me. I would not look in Matt's direction.

'Be nice to each other. You're both good men, and good men should…' I didn't finish. What was I trying to say, that they should be friends?

Matt dragged on his cigarette, hard, before grinding it into the sand. He looked ready to spit the taste of me out, but he said, 'Anything you say, Prophet. Anything you say.' An uneasy alliance.

I was down on the beach like a shot, even before Grant turned his car around. Like a distant miracle Leo lifted his arm and waved me forward. When I reached him I repeated the words that Grant had said to me, 'You okay?'

'Come and watch the sun go down, Mum. God's about to blink a green eye on the horizon. Tell me who those two men were.'

I immediately dropped Matt out of the equation. 'The older one is my husband, Grant, which I guess, makes him your stepfather.' I sucked clean air into my lungs. 'You have a brother and sister, too. Their names are Ty and Charity.'

He sat quietly and absorbed it. 'And the other one?'

'The guy who runs the pub.'

I knew there might never be a better time to tell him about the kids, his siblings, and never a better place, yet I had no wish to spoil his affinity with this particular spot. But I had the profound feeling that perhaps it would sound less terrible, less of a betrayal, to tell him here of his replacements. I kept the story brief.

My mother believed in the power of goodness and she kept the faith for almost a year, turning it on and off like a tap. 'We'll get the boy back,' she'd tell me. 'You'll see. Things like this don't happen to good people.'

I thought that a strange statement coming from her. So why was she always so sick?

She said, 'Rick doesn't deserve him and we do. He doesn't love him like we do. Leo will come home, mark my words. We'll find him. We'll get him back, you wait and see.'

But as hope steadily deserted, swirling like so much dirty water down the Pirongia kitchen drain, I watched her shrinking, week by week. Even so, her loss of buoyancy caught me by surprise. It was only after she'd been taken away, for what turned out to be a short course of palliative care, that the doctor told me. Cancer. Of course. It had started in her breast.

Jenny had known, he said. 'Why make me have me an operation that comes too late to save me? Why take medicine that only makes you sick?'

Sometimes being practical can kill you, and sometimes it can save you. Jenny had thrown her dice, and she'd lost. And immediately after the funeral, I'd made an appointment in Te Kuiti, at the bank. I'd asked someone I didn't know to lend me money. Then eventually I'd gone out and found two jobs, both lowly and badly paid, one in the morning and one at night. But mopping the Otorohanga Motel floors was better than doing nothing, and wiping tables at Oscar's Café proved I was still alive.

But even with Grant on board, we'd failed to find my son. The trail went cold in Sydney and never warmed up again.

I didn't want a husband, but handing the reins to someone else had meant that I survived. I didn't want a baby either, no way, not ever again. I told myself that I would never make myself vulnerable like that again. The loss of another child would just about nail my emotional coffin shut.

But then I missed a period almost immediately after Grant and I married, and this time I knew what it meant. Despite my inhibitions, I experienced, in addition to the sense of a door swinging shut, little by little and soundlessly, an unexpected leap of my heart. I felt an extreme readiness to hold out my arms. If I was destined to have this child, if God wanted me to, then He would not be so cruel as to let anything take the child from me.

And that was Ty, whose name was a nod at the ties that bind. And Ty had helped to heal me.

And fourteen months later, when Charity was born, she helped heal me too. I called Charity for no better reason than my mother had called me Cassandra – just a mother who liked the name.

Ty's birth had been bittersweet, but Charity's had brought such joy. They'd grown up in a continuing drama, one they knew nothing at all about.

'I think, for the first few years, I was so busy it was okay,' I told Leo. 'But lately…' Lately things had changed and the kids no longer helped. Things were slipping, like the rollers in Jenny's old wringer washing machine. And lately, if I was to be honest, meant not the last six or seven months, but possibly the last six or seven years, from around the time when Ty turned ten, when, probably, old scar tissue had started to grow.

My God.

'They weren't replacements,' I said to Leo. 'But once they were born I loved them nearly as much as you.' Nearly?

Leo said, 'I always knew you loved me. How old were you when you had me? I'm not sure I've ever known.'

'Fifteen.'

'That's both sad and terrible. But it explains some of the things we did, how much you enjoyed your games.'

My games? For a second, I wasn't sure what he meant, and then for one single brilliant light-bulb moment I thought impossibly, maybe, yes. We'd played everything from Boston tea parties to the Battle of Waterloo. Everyone from Batman to the Scarlet Pimpernel. I was the lonely child of a lonely woman, so yes, I'd enjoyed our games.

Perhaps we're finally getting somewhere, I thought, edging closer to some truth I didn't have any understanding for, getting a grip on perhaps a reason why Rick might have done what he did. I remembered that look on his face. It had carried such anger and disgust.

'Enough, enough, already!' Leo slapped his forehead hard, as though trying to get himself out once more from under the weight of our combined history. He tugged me to my feet. My legs felt like sinkers, but everything else, incredibly, seemed to weigh less. Yes, we were getting somewhere, in the process of pulling ourselves apart so we could get us fixed.

'Let's go, we've got a party on, remember,' Leo said, sounding eight or nine, as though he was carrying a birthday cake to Jenny on one of her best china plates, from a Pirongia lean-to kitchen through to a high-stud Pirongia lounge.

Chapter Twenty-one

We negotiated the road to the party at Ngawi as though it was the one we drove every day to the mall. The sun had set and all that was visible in the early night was the guano on the top of the Black Rocks. I knew the landscape now, even in the darkness. I no longer felt such a stranger.

'How much do these people know about us?'

'Not much and it doesn't matter. Many of the people out here have interesting pasts.' Though he said interesting, I heard the word wretched.

'It's coming up on the left,' Leo said. 'After the next bend you should see the lights.'

I imagined he meant the lights from the baches scattered on the hill, lit up like glow-worms on a bank. No need to pull curtains in a pigeon loft, I thought. But he pointed to a lone shack down by the water's edge, coloured lights strung beneath the eaves blinking a clear welcome.

'Pull in here.'

I stopped the car on kikuyu, dark sand showing through like liver spots on skin. There were a lot of other vehicles parked around.

'Come and meet the gang,' Leo said. He opened the car door for me and groaned when I pocketed the keys. 'Put them back in the ignition, Mum. What kind of people do you think these are?'

I followed him down another path of crazy paving, while the night began to reassemble into real and proper shapes. Dark figures sat around on a low deck, their laughter carrying a long way in the stillness. Comfort was followed suddenly by a peculiar kind of envy

– they were all part of this, I thought, as integral and binding as the smell from the sea. There was still no wind, there'd been none all day, but I could taste it – salt, sand, sea and other people's lives.

A man came up to shake my hand. He wore an old flannel shirt, sleeves rolled up to his elbows, and a fishing hat jammed low over his eyes. His lips shone iridescent, two small sprats, and spittle flew out when he spoke.

'Yo, Leo!' He laughed, though he was shaking my hand so hard it almost hurt.

'Jans. This is Cass. My mother. My mother, Cass.'

It registered, even thrilled me, that he'd said it all three ways. I'd wondered how he'd do it and now I felt ridiculously stoked. I watched one of Jan's eyebrows jump, but that was all.

'Welcome! Beer or smoke or both?'

'Definitely a beer.'

I realised now that the smell of dope hung like a damp net over everything, so thick it could capture insects and send them wasted to the ground.

'Make it two beers,' Leo said. 'I'm so thirsty I'd drink from a dead sailor's shoe. Well, any dead sailor's except yours.'

'Okay, then,' the man said. 'Three beers. One for you and two for your mother here.'

'Two sails to the wind already,' Leo said in a stage whisper. 'What kind of a state is this to meet my mother, Jans?'

Jans still gripped my hand and laughed again as he shook it even harder than before.

'Fucking glad to meet you, girl. You look so fucking alike, if you'll excuse my French, more like his sister.'

'Do we really look alike? Do we?' I was excited by the thought and as happy as a child at Christmas given exactly the thing she wants. I hadn't stopped to think about it. Fifteen years between us. I guessed, physically, it wasn't much of a chasm. Family resemblances are better read by those who know you least, that's what Jenny once said.

'If he'd just get rid of this,' the man said, tugging on Leo's long hair, 'you'd be two peas in a fucking pod. You looked in the mirror lately? Hell, I guess not.'

He passed the beers across. The bottles were cool and slippery in my fingers. I handed one to Leo and rolled mine across my brow.

'I feel bad coming here empty-handed,' I said.

'Don't be stupid,' Jans said. He pointed a hairy knuckle at Leo. 'Who do you reckon supplied the crays? We kept them in a tank for a week. Went out early in case the weather turned to crap.'

'Really?'

'We'll cook them up in seawater soon and eat the bastards hot.'

A kind of ancient pride rolled into me like thunder: to eat warm crayfish your own child had gleaned from the rocks, under the stars on a balmy night…

'Come and meet the rest of the crew. They'll be wondering where you've been hiding.'

We went from group to group, and I was introduced. Genuine smiles followed and not a single question asked. It wouldn't have happened at a work do in the city, I knew, not this kind of easy acceptance. There'd be all those visits to the ladies in pairs to swap that particular brand of party gossip everyone got so good at. Well, perhaps I'll never go back, I thought. No one was indispensable. Perhaps I'd return just long enough to pack up my desk, thumb my nose at the whole lot of them. 'I'm leaving. Going south. See, you all live happily in your black power suits. Me? I'm going to live. In dirty Levis till I die.'

But then over the ocean came Charity's plaintive cry. 'Don't forget the ball.' And a phone in my head began to ring and it was Ty being responsible, saying, 'Come and pick me up. I've been drinking.' And Grant whispering from his chair, half-asleep, 'I want you to meet us for lunch, tomorrow, don't forget. I want you to impress my clients with your clever wit and charm.'

Like bugs, I shook the images off and followed Leo to the end of a loose timber deck. We'd lost Jans somewhere along the way. Despite his flattery, I was pleased to have him gone and Leo to myself again. With muscles beginning to seriously seize from the lighthouse climb, I tried not to mind the discomfort as I sat down. I'd learn to jog those stairs, given time.

A figure came up from the beach.

'Leo!' The female voice rang out, loud and strong. 'What took you so damn long! Where you been?' The delight was obvious. The tone was young but the silhouetted body tall and wide as she put her hands into the small of her back and flexed, before clapping one over each of Leo's ears to pull him forward, make him kiss her on the mouth. Her eyes reflected light from the nearest bulb – yellow.

'Whoa!' Leo said. 'This is Ngaia.'

'Ngaia with the mokopuna in her friggin big puku,' the girl said.

There's this girl I know in Ngawi. Thinks she has a sense of humour… No mention of the kind of relationship that would, or could, produce a child.

'And who might you be, hey?' Ngaia demanded.

'Don't be so rude,' Leo said pleasantly. 'Say hello to my mother.'

The girl swung her full gaze on me. 'My, aren't we the best-kept little secret in town.'

'You just assumed I didn't have one,' Leo said. 'Lots of water under lots of bridges. It's just that Mum and I haven't seen each other for a few years.'

'More than a few, actually,' I said, though why it had to come out sounding prim and proper, I didn't know. I felt the absurd desire to thrust my arm through Ngaia's, drag her out of this place, out under a proper streetlight and say, 'Hands off, he's mine. I've only just found him and I'm not ready to give him up.'

But the girl simply smiled. 'I dare say the story's long and boring, yeah?'

Leo chose not to answer. 'What have you been doing down the beach?'

'Oh, nothing scandalous. Not digging up long-lost rellies or anything like that. More praying to the Goddess of Birth for safe passage, that sort of thing.' Her face became suddenly sly, yet when she began to speak again she sounded innocent, like a child. 'What's her name again, Hinetitama or something?'

'Hine-te-iwaiwa,' Leo said, the fat syllables slipping easily off his tongue. 'At least that's what you've been telling me for weeks. Stop trying to catch me out. You've probably been walking on the water, or trying to.'

'A spiritual name,' she said, ignoring him completely. 'A name that means something. Not just any old name like Leo.'

Leo is not just any old name, I thought. But I said, 'How long have you got to go?' Thinking there's no real reason why I can't be polite, why I can't pretend I want to know.

'No idea. I'm overdue.' Fingers caressed a stomach, above and below the mound. The gesture was oddly disconcerting, borderline obscene. I expected her hands to come up, cup both breasts, weigh them. 'I'm very overdue. Ripe.'

The word made me wince. 'Well, I don't suppose the doctor will let you go more than two weeks past your due date.' And there it was again, that snobbish, superior ring. 'It can't be too much longer.'

'No, I guess not, but bugger the doctor,' the girl said. 'That's what I've got Leo for, right Leo? To get this baby born.' She stood straighter now, as though she was some fresh young sapling poked into the sand at our feet and watered long enough to take root.

All I felt was fear. I tried to take her in, all of her, from the tips of her feet to the top of her uncombed head. Ngaia had dreadlocks, long and even, as though all the rest in the world were minor, lesser copies. Ropes of perfect thickness, they were woven here and there with beads and shells. She'd pushed a feather into her crown where it stuck up high enough to give her a ghostly, warrior look.

A seagull feather. I'd done that myself, as a child, stuck a feather behind an ear, though it had had no real significance except a kid's wish not to waste a treasure. But on Ngaia it was somehow different – there was an arrogance about it, as though something as delicate as a feather could wedge open the sky and earth and keep her balanced in the middle.

Her eyes, like her face, were substantial, dark and almond-shaped. The clothes she wore looked ethnic – a sarong knotted above her breasts, a clean white cotton shirt opened down the front, like a boy's.

'She thinks she can just squat down in the dunes when her time comes,' Leo said. 'Don't you, Ngaia?'

'Sure, why not. Like all good wahines. He mihi. E nga reo, e nga mana, e nga hau e wha…'

'Don't be fooled,' Leo turned to me. 'She got that from a book. She doesn't speak the language, just drops the odd word in now and again to make the rest of us feel ignorant. It's all part of the reverse journey she thinks she's on, from the new world back into the old.'

A bubble of glee rose up from Ngaia like a belch. 'Oh you! Bugger you! And bugger the old wahines too! So long as I've got you to hold my hand, and a paua shell to cut the cord, I'll be right, e Tane?'

A shiver ran up my spine and stopped just short of my neck. Something passed between them, Ngaia and Leo, a certain shimmering something that could have been placed anywhere on the broad spectrum of love. At first I felt lifted up, then slammed back down hard. It was personal, so personal it excluded me. I watched the colours bleed from the lights overhead.

'Leo,' I began, but Leo wasn't listening. He held Ngaia's eyes while Ngaia laughed again. But to me it didn't feel like laughing, more like she was spitting in my face.

'You'll manage,' the girl said. 'It'll be just like gutting fish.'

Chapter Twenty-two

I sat cross-legged on the ground and ate my crayfish, saying thank you, thank you, thank you, to generous Jans. But all the while my head dropped further down, with an emotion that keep changing shape. It was ugly, and I couldn't control it. I'd been cheated, I'd been robbed. I'd been lied to by the lighthouse and the land. I'd been sucked in by my own fantasies. I'd believed all I had to do was find him and he'd be mine alone. How dumb could I be? He wasn't mine at all, not to keep, just lent for a couple of days.

New sorrow tore into me and subsided. It wasn't jealousy. I couldn't be jealous of Ngaia, not an unknown pregnant girl. It was this new claim to him that now negated mine, and something else that whispered in my ear, 'History repeats, repeats.'

'Tineke's inside,' Leo said, coming up behind me quietly and putting his hand on my back, as though he knew the best thing he could do for me, at that moment, was touch me. 'She'll be ruling the roost somewhere. I'd like you to come and meet her.'

'I don't think I can stand up properly. My legs are so sore.' I sounded what I was, a drained, petulant woman.

'You tourist,' Leo chuckled. 'Come closer to the fire. The warmth will help. I'll bring Tineke out in a minute.'

I moved closer to a fire that could never warm me up. Started in a barbecue pit on the ground with more wood added, it didn't lack embers, but I couldn't feel the sparks. 'Leo, I think I should get going soon. Back to the pub.' I'd stopped pining for a happy ending.

'What's the time?'

'It's almost ten. I'm really tired. I've had a hard day,' I thought, pathetic and sorry for myself. 'I've had a hard week.'

Sad to think that the knowledge it craved could wear a body out.

Leo came closer to the fire, closer to me, warming his big hands up over the fast diminishing logs. Anyone else would have had a mark on his wrist to show where a watch had gone, but Leo's arm was only brown. He'd given it away, he told me, the day he arrived in the bay.

I remembered now, how I'd told Grant I'd take Leo back with me, to meet him properly, but it didn't seem right, to front up with some pregnant girlfriend too. All I wanted to do right now, was fall asleep in a pile, go to bed and have Grant snore beside me.

'What about the funeral?' I asked. 'Are you certain you won't go?'

'Absolutely,' Leo said.

There was no earthly reason for me to go without him, but if he wanted me to go on his behalf, I would.

'If you'd like me to go in your place, then I will.'

'No. I don't care if you go or not. It's up to you. Is the funeral a deadline for leaving the bay?'

It had been, but now I didn't know.

'Leo, there are still things I need to know about. Things we both need to know.'

He sensed my melancholy. 'I know. Whatever you do, please don't rush away without saying goodbye, without telling me. Please don't just leave.'

'No. I won't.' No cut, lick and spit. No promise. 'What might be the chances, do you think, of you making it over to the pub for breakfast? Grant wants to meet you. Bring Ngaia if she wants to come.' It sounded so reluctant, even in my own ears, I was ashamed. 'I could whizz back first thing and pick you up.'

I didn't think I was capable of whizzing anywhere.

'I don't know, Mum.' Leo said slowly. 'I'll have to check. Ngaia might have different plans.'

On the way back to the pub, alone in the car, I made another pact with God. Give him to me for just one more day, and I'll let him go in peace, back to Ngaia. Then I'd go back to selling real estate and simply get on with things. History had proved I was very good at that as well.

Outside the Lake Ferry there were two cars – Grant's and someone else's. I parked mine between them, climbed slowly up the steps to the door. As if for punishment, my legs were now so heavy I should have crawled. Voices came from the bar.

I knew to find my husband I'd have to go in and say hello. And there at one end of the counter stood Grant and Matt looking really chummy, with a new couple at the other, the woman, not much older than me, wearing impossibly high-heeled shoes, the man, slightly younger, in a worn but classy jacket.

I took an instant dislike to the woman. Possibly it was all the make-up she had on, as though she'd got ready in front of a mirror in a darkened room. Possibly, it was just my frame of mind.

'Here she is at last. Here is Cass,' Grant said. 'And Leo? Is he with you?'

I shook my head, wanting to have him hold me, steer me down the hall and roll me into bed, turn my prickles to the world like a hedgehog. Three sets of curious eyes fell on me.

'Here she is indeed,' Matt said. 'Welcome back, Prophet.' There was something in his tone, but I couldn't read it. I wondered if he'd had too much to drink. 'And in time to meet my mother before she goes to bed.'

The woman barely nodded in my direction, before going immediately back to talking animatedly to the man, who so obviously did not come from these parts.

'I'll introduce myself,' he said shoving a thick wad of fingers out. 'Phil Phillips. Pleased to meet you.'

I'd know your type anywhere, I thought. Used cars or insurance?

Over the top of the heads, Matt rolled his eyes. 'Mum's latest catch,' he mouthed, the way he'd mouthed 'beer' on Wednesday night across a room of stranded anglers.

There was an awkward silence until Grant rescued us all. 'If you will excuse us, we will say good night. Cass looks tired and she has things to talk about.'

'I just bet she has,' Matt said.

I held on to Grant's arm as though I would fall through space if I wasn't anchored down. In the car, I'd made more than one pact with God. I'd made several. Don't let Grant find out about the morning of the storm, and I'll never mention Julie Weston's name again. Let me off the hook and I'll let Grant off too. I'll make everything up to everyone, the kids as well, if you just let me keep them and not take anyone away.

As he bent to open our bedroom door, Grant stopped. 'Cassie. Do you have something the matter with your legs?'

Not just my legs. 'Today I climbed to a lighthouse and now they hurt like hell.'

'I'll run you a bath.'

'I don't think there is a bath,' I said. At least, I hadn't seen one. 'And please stop babying me.' It was the last speck of residual anger and fear. I didn't want a bath. Grant might see me naked, the scarlet letter on my skin.

'I'm sorry. I'm just so tired,' I said. 'I just want to go to bed.'

'I don't know what you have done to that young man,' Grant said. 'Matt. So full of this prophet thing. For some reason he seems immensely curious about you.'

By the time I climbed into bed with Grant only the fear remained.

Chapter Twenty-three

It was Saturday morning when I stepped out through the french doors, just in time to see a small four-wheel drive hurtling down the road and up onto the gravel in front of the hotel. It was a little upright thing, a black box on wheels, but it looked in better nick than most of the cars I'd so far seen around Lake Ferry, many of which would never pass a warrant.

'It's the salt air. Kills cars around here,' Matt had said. 'Laurel changes hers every time the wind blows. Gives her a good excuse to go into town.'

Ah, I thought, so that's where she found him. Under some flapping triangular flags, not in a broker's office.

The vehicle stopped as close to the pub as possible, without actually driving up the stairs. When I realised who was driving, I waved excitedly. 'Leo!'

Grant appeared on the porch beside me.

I said, 'Look who's come for breakfast!' Then I watched as Leo bounced from the driver's seat and threw open the passenger door.

'And look,' I said, not quite so excitedly, 'he's brought Ngaia.'

'Ngaia?' Grant said. 'Who's Ngaia.'

I bit back the urge to say, 'Well, Ngaia is Ngaia.'

Ngaia emerged like a fat brown caterpillar from the small black cocoon. Leo leaned into the vehicle, wrenched the front seat forward and unfolded someone else from the back – an old woman, bent and awkward, in a long dark skirt that flowed around her ankles and a cane that went deep into the ground.

'So who is that?'

'I'm not sure, but I think that's Tineke.'

The old woman yelled out gaily across the car park. 'Better get ourselves introduced in a hurry, eh! Going to get us a mokopuna today!'

Grant looked lost. Last night, I had told him some of what I'd learnt but only up to mid-way through the party, which deliberately left Ngaia out. I'd left Tineke out too. If Matt had been around I might have let him say it was Freudian, because it was.

'I didn't just find a son, but a partner and a baby as well.'

'I beg your pardon?'

And then I went inside, leaving Grant and his questions behind, and raced through the pub to the front door.

'Morning!' Leo said, as soon as he saw me. 'Told you she's stubborn when she wants to be. We could have got her into the Hutt Valley if she'd told us in time.'

The old woman cackled. 'Could have got her over there, but wouldn't have made her stick. She'd have come back, thumb out, big belly out too, hitching. This one's been awake all night while yous was snoring. Always said she'd have her baby in the bay. Can't blame her really, or this boy, wanting to stay close to his Nanny.'

'What's this "boy" business,' Ngaia wheezed. 'Told you, Nan, it's a girl.'

The old woman scraped a long dark finger down an equally long dark nose, before tapping on Ngaia's stomach. 'What I know, I know, and this here's a boy.'

She smiled good-naturedly at me, and then at Grant as he came up behind me. 'I'm Tineke, eh. Pleased to meet yous. This here's Ngaia, my granddaughter, she's a pain in the bum.'

'Don't talk to me about pain,' Ngaia said as she doubled over.

Then Leo stepped in beside them and offered them both an arm. It was such a valiant gesture. I would put my anguish away and concentrate on Ngaia, if my legs would let me, and try to help this baby to be born. The old woman accepted Leo's arm eagerly but the girl declined. 'Don't start thinking I need you yet, e tane, I'll tell you when.'

Then Matt arrived from somewhere, with Laurel following like a rottweiler.

'She can't just drop her sprog here, this is a public house!'

I heard Matt snort behind me. 'Bit early in the day to be issuing last orders,' he said.

'How many kids yous got?' Tineke leaned in and asked us all. I expected to feel her finger in my ribs. For the first time in my life I answered truthfully and without panic. 'I've got three.'

Her gaze fell like a net over Laurel, 'How many yous got, eh?'

'She got lumbered with just the one,' Matt said.

Was that really how Laurel had made him feel? Like she'd been stuck with him against her will?

'Well, I got eight,' Tineke said. 'That makes twelve between us. I reckon we should be able to get the job done.'

Laurel's jaw dropped further as she looked around for rescue. 'Where's Phil? Who's seen Phil? Phil!' she called, going back the way she'd been. Her face looked anxious, as though she'd shut her eyes for sixty seconds and he'd thoughtlessly disappeared.

'Better find him quick and nail his feet to the floor,' Matt said loud enough for me to hear. 'Or he'll be like all the rest and only last a week.'

Then Grant advanced, like a good rearguard, to get us all in line.

'Right. Who is who around here? You must be Leo. Finally, we meet,' and he stepped forward, held Leo to his chest in such a way that it made my blood go thick. He kept his grip longer than I expected, and when he pushed Leo out, it was to look at him again.

'I can see the family resemblance,' Grant said, swinging his gaze on me. 'You and your mother.'

'Yes, we know,' Leo said. 'We've been told.'

I wondered about the baby – would he be the third pea in the pod?

Grant continued to look at me and I realised his eyes were wet. 'Finally,' he said to me. 'Finally.'

'And Leo, this is Matt. Matt, Leo, my eldest son.' I wanted to introduce Leo as well as he had introduced me to Jans last night.

'Heard heaps about you, man. Good to meet you,' Matt said, and thumped him on the chin.

And then we all stood there in silence, like a five-sided fairy ring, until Tineke said, rather grandly, 'And don't forget I'm Tineke', and made us all laugh.

Laurel came back, towing Phil like a small reluctant schooner being dragged by an almighty barge. He looked rumpled, as though he'd been unexpectedly pulled from his sheets. 'Look at them. Do something – they think they can just waltz in here and drop a baby on my carpet.'

Phil didn't say a word, but stood like a television with the sound turned off.

'It won't be on the carpet, Laurel,' Matt said. 'We don't want to endanger the kid before he's taken his first breath. It'll be in a bed. Prophet, you come with me and help me choose one.'

'Thank you,' I murmured, as I followed him down the hallway. 'Thank you so very much, Matt.'

'What for? It's nice to have a decent part to play in all this drama, even if it is along with half the bay.'

'I didn't mean that. The best room would be one on the seaward side,' I said. 'Like ours. With doors.' I knew instinctively that Ngaia would prefer a room where she could see the lagoon.

'Now, tell me you've delivered a baby before.'

'Only my own and I don't imagine that counts.'

'Don't worry. I'm sure you'll remember the moves. But don't count on Laurel for anything, Prophet, not even good grace. Sometimes I think she found me at the bottom of a keg and thought, "What on earth is this for? I don't know what it is, but it might come in handy." But, far out, your Grant looks like a useful tool.'

I thought of Grant's capable hands shuffling papers on a desk, knowing exactly where to put them in the filing cabinet, but not sure whether to file this one under B for baby or D for delivery. 'Yes, he is. But I honestly don't how he'll manage here. He's a bit out of his depth.'

'Him and me both,' Matt said, 'and probably Leo as well, but leave it to me. If it gets too much for us manly dudes, I'll open the bar.'

We went through the last door. The room was light and airy. 'This one, then.'

He went off to fetch Ngaia and her entourage while I put new linen on the bed.

The first thing Ngaia said was, 'You're not getting me into no bed.' Eventually she conceded to having the mattress dragged onto the floor. Matt and Grant carried the frame out and stood it up in the hall as Laurel's face came round the corner of the door like a judgement. 'You can bloody well clean up your own mess when you've finished.'

I looked at Matt in sympathy. Was this how it was? How it had always been?

Chapter Twenty-four

I took up position beside Tineke, who sat in a straight-backed chair with the nape of her neck pressed against the wall. Though her eyes were shut, they worked beneath her lids. A smile played loosely on her lips, and she seemed exactly the way Leo had described her, queenly, almost regal, with her cane tapping gently against one side of her foot. I admired her for a long time. She should have worn a moko on her chin – it would have suited her.

Leo moved the mattress closer to the doors and into a square of sunlight. I heard Ngaia sigh, 'Argh. I feel like a patient.'

I looked across to Leo, who stared back in return. I wondered if he was thinking, as I was, how odd it is to finish our reunion like this. In life we are in death, Jenny might have said, only this time it had been the other way around.

'Just go with the flow, girl, as long as you can,' Tineke said, without opening her eyes. 'Takes a hundred and fifty of those contractions to get you a baby.'

'If you say give or take a few, Nan, I'll bloody kill you.'

But Tineke was right. You could count off a hundred and fifty contractions to deliver a baby. At the age of twenty-nine, giving birth to Ty, I'd known more than the doctor who looked all of twenty-three. When I had accidentally tested his knowledge by asking him things he didn't know, he'd shut me up by saying through his nose, 'This is your pregnancy, Mrs McClellan, not mine.'

But unlike that long ago day when Leo was born with only Jenny in attendance, Grant had been the first one to hold the baby. We'd gone home as a family. I hadn't passed the buck to Jenny and returned to being a child.

And now here was Leo, about to have a child of his own. I watched him walk the room with Ngaia, so sensitive to her needs, gliding her past the mattress corners so she wouldn't trip.

An unusual relationship, I thought. Full of affection, but…I wasn't sure. Something was missing.

'Oh, Nan,' Ngaia cried out.

'Good girl,' Tineke said quietly. 'Good girl, darling, you walk.'

'Why are you bloody whispering? No one's bloody died.'

Wrong, I thought. But the more I thought of Rick, the less effect he had on me. Once the mention of his name thrust a knife into my veins but the blade was growing blunt and less effective.

'I want a drink of water,' Ngaia said.

'I'll get it.'

In the kitchen I found Matt and Grant, sitting at a table drinking coffee.

'God,' I said. 'They're probably full of rum.'

'No, not yet, but they might be soon,' Grant said. 'I think we might need something stronger by the time this day is out.'

'Way out here on the peripheral and you two only fringe-dwellers?'

'Well, why not?' They were conspirators. 'This happens to be a pub.'

I found a large beer jug behind a cupboard door and filled it with water.

'See? Thirsty work,' Matt said.

Back in the room I poured a drink for Ngaia first, then Leo.

'I don't know why, but even the water tastes better here in the bay.'

'It's rainwater. Like at home.'

It took me a moment to realise he meant with Jenny and me.

Outside the sun had moved over the yardarm, over the roof, and the lake was calm.

'How goes it? Te whakamamae o te whaea? The labour of the mother?' the old woman asked after a while.

'Ask me something else. I don't know nothing,' Ngaia said. 'Not today.'

'It won't happen overnight but it will happen, eh? Don't you worry, girl, I'll listen out for your grunts. Remember, old and wise? We know what I know.'

It was only a couple of minutes until the next contraction hit.

'Nan! Oh hell, Nan!'

The pains were coming faster in definite waves.

'Maybe you should lie down,' Leo suggested. 'A rest might do you good. What do you think?'

'I think you're full of crap, that's what,' Ngaia snapped.

And then her labour stopped.

'Feels like someone's yanked my bloody batteries out,' she complained. For the first time, Tineke eased herself up out of her chair. She tapped her cane against the mattress. 'This is a good thing. Give you a break. You curl up there, darling, and I'll curl up too, have a sleep beside you. Listen while you slumber.'

She sent Leo on a mission. 'Go boil water like in the old days, boy. We'll bellow if we want you.'

'Like a wounded bull,' Ngaia said.

We made a woman's pledge, one that could be trusted, that we'd call him back if and when things progressed. In the end he went without too much arguing, off to the kitchen to join the other men. I took up Tineke's watching position against the wall. We didn't get to call Leo back for another hour.

Ngaia woke in a panic. 'I've gone and wet myself!'

Tineke woke more slowly, and took her hand. 'Your waters have broken. Things will go quickly now – might soon be over.'

We shouted out for Leo.

But for another hour and then another, Ngaia squirmed and moaned, on her knees, on the floor, against the walls, against anybody who would have her. She wanted Leo, she loved Leo, Leo was the man. When Grant put in an appearance, as did Matt, it was obvious they weren't going to fit the bill and they fled for the kitchen again.

Ngaia was fast losing her grip on the contractions. Labour had removed not only the last of her resistance, but all her clothes as well. She had thrown them off as soon as she'd found them wet. It didn't seem to matter to anyone, and even I had to acknowledge that Ngaia looked smooth and gorgeous, even squatting with the pains.

'No one made you lie down in the old days. Or wear man-made crap over your bones.'

'You're right. It was the medical profession who decided women should be horizontal,' I agreed. 'They were the ones who raised the beds so doctors wouldn't have to bend.'

Ngaia's head rose up. Leo blotted her brow with her discarded sarong.

'Really?'

'Yes, really.'

'So this is truly the right way?'

'I guess so.'

'I knew it,' Ngaia was triumphant. 'These are my tupuna pulling my strings.'

It was Sunday, two o'clock – Rick would be buried this time tomorrow – when Ngaia began to push. Tineke was back in her chair and wide awake.

Leo began to give out quiet orders as he held Ngaia over the mattress on the floor. 'Listen to your tupuna, breathe for them. You can do it. You can do it. Didn't I always tell you you were clever? You are a warrior, you are a warrior woman, you can push this baby out.' He was behind her, holding her, knowing gravity would help. His voice came out staccato, full of concern.

I loved him so much at that moment I almost split in half. In spite of all that Rick had put him through, he had managed to retain his acute awareness of others. As a child he'd always known exactly what Jenny or I were feeling.

Now his chin grazed Ngaia's dreadlocks. He tried to smile at me but, like mine at times, his smile didn't match his eyes. I knew what he was thinking because I was thinking it too. We're in the middle of a miracle. But it's only a miracle if it turns out okay.

Ngaia pushed and pushed again. The noises she made were formed deep in her throat.

Tineke pointed at me with her stick. 'Catch the baby.'

'I can't.'

'Have to. Aue, I'm no good, I'm too old, might drop it.' She pointed to Leo. 'He can't do it, he's too busy.'

I looked helplessly at Ngaia.

'It's okay, Leo's mother. You do it,' she said.

Obediently, I got down on the mattress, and almost before my knees touched, the baby plunged into my lap, plum-coloured, wet and oozing and as waxy as a crayon. I knew immediately what I wanted to do with it: shove it up my jumper, put it against my bare skin.

'Now,' I heard Tineke say, 'give the baby to its mother.'

'Leo,' I whispered. 'Leo.'

His child lay across my knees, fat and sticky with its strong earthy smell but in that instant it was mine. Was this how Jenny had felt when Leo was born? Is this why she'd taken over?

Tineke said again, 'Give that child to its mother.' She began to rise from her chair. I expected her to grab me by the hair, snatch the baby and pass it over where it belonged, to Ngaia, but instead she threw a paua shell onto the bed.

Without changing position, Leo took the shell and drew it hard across the cord, gently took the child from me and gave him to his mother.

Tineke broke the bad news. 'It's a boy.'

'Well, what a big surprise, Nan,' Ngaia said, collapsing back on the bed, holding the baby to her breast. 'Of course, I knew it all along. I was only having you on, old woman.' She touched the wrinkled head. 'I think I'm going to call you Kutukutu Iti, little maggot.'

'You wouldn't,' the old woman said.

'Wouldn't I?'

'He's the wrong colour,' Tineke sniffed. 'Not too much white in him.'

And it was true, something I had yet to make sense of. The baby's skin was darker than Ngaia's, not the same colour at all, much deeper, like black taffeta.

'Okay, so Little Maggot has been ruled out,' she told the baby. 'So how about Tauho Iti – little stranger? Well, it's true, Nan, we don't know where he came from so how can we know who he is.'

Little stranger?

I looked to where Leo sat, next to Ngaia on the bed. Tears ran in rivers down his face. I wanted to go to him and kiss it better, wipe the tears away but my hands were covered in vernix, and of course, my legs had locked.

'Welcome to the world, Tauho Iti,' Leo said.

I knew Tineke watched me sharply as a morepork on a branch. I raised my head and dared her not to speak. But a look passed between us, something old and very fleeting, but I knew exactly what was said. Poor you.

Then the old kuia dropped her head and began her song of welcome. 'Nau mai ra e te tau e ko koe ra te puawaitanga…' but to me it sounded more like a lament.

I picked up the instrument that had cut the cord and turned it over and over in my hands. Inside, the colours shone as bright as ever. On the sharp edge lay a single drop of blood.

'I'll take this,' I said. 'Have something made for the baby.'

Ngaia's mouth was soft and generous. 'Nah. Go on, you keep it,' she said.

Chapter Twenty-five

'Wake up, old woman! It was me who did all the work, so how come you're the one sleeping!' Ngaia dropped her chin down onto her chest, nuzzled the baby. 'Me and Tauho Iti, we feel very lucky.'

Leo spoke for us all. 'So do we.'

I looked outside the window. It had to be nearly four o'clock.

'Fancy a walk, Leo? Along the beach?' We could tell the others on the way.

'Your legs all right?'

'The walk will do me good.'

'I'll look after these two,' Tineke said. 'Take your son and go.'

'Hey!' Ngaia called after us, 'come back. Suppose you want Suki back now, eh Leo?'

'Suki?'

'Suki the Suzuki,' Leo said. 'It's a joke. I lent it to Ngaia in case she needed a vehicle in a hurry. No shortage of volunteer drivers in the bay. No. You keep it.'

'Christening present,' he added, as we wandered down the hall. 'Well, she needs it more than I do. She's got nothing. Let's go give the kitchen cowards the good news and then we'll get out of here and I'll tell you anything you want to know.'

In the kitchen, Matt was standing at the bench, peeling potatoes, while Grant chopped them into chips. Grant wore an old striped apron, like some chunky school matron.

Matt said. 'Real men cook.'

I remembered the meals Grant had made when I was sick, and

more recently, the ones Leo had made without even a frying pan.

'Yes. Real men cook.'

Matt, full of good humour, said, 'Who is this woman? I like this woman.'

'And if anyone wants to know, it's a boy. Very big. Very healthy.' And very very black.

Matt put down his knife. 'And who might the proud father be?'

'Long story,' Leo said, 'but it's not me.'

Grant put down his knife too. 'After dinner, I thought I would head back to Auckland, Cassie, drive through the night. I think someone should go to the funeral. Rick might not have been much of a man but he gave us Leo. I think someone in the family should go and bear witness. I think it should be me.'

For a second I hoped he had been to bed with a dozen wild women, because he deserved so much more than just me. Maybe one day we could swap notes and still survive.

Leo stood quietly, back against the table.

'Leo?'

'It seems a very noble idea.' Then he was animated, impatient, full of business. 'Let's walk,' he said to me.

Where would we go, except, of course, along the rim of the lagoon, where I kept hearing Grant's words in the air all around me. 'He gave us Leo.'

The wind was light, but with a muddy edge, and I felt as though we were in the middle of a brand new spring. The wind was quiet, the waves low, and I knew the sun would go down very soon, I felt certain we'd see one of Palliser's famous sunsets – a gift for Tauho Iti's birthday.

By some silent mutual agreement, we wandered along past the pastel baches.

'I worked in Wellington,' Leo said, digging his heels in the sand, the way kids always do, to make those dragging patterns. 'I taught English to the kids who fell through the cracks. That's how I met Ngaia. She's a good kid, but brought up by people who didn't seem to care. I taught her for a year. Reading, writing and non-curriculum arithmetic. She even stopped saying yous.' He looked sideways at me. 'Then one day she came to me, and she was a mess. Got wasted at some party and a whole lot of guys…' He searched for a better word than the one he had in mind, but then he gave up and used it. 'Well, I'm sure you know what happened. She was gang-banged, raped.

'Apart from the obvious tragedy of the thing, the timing was terrible,' Leo said. 'She'd been working so hard, and we'd been making good ground. When she came to tell me she was dropping out I made her promise to stick it out, at least till the end of the term.'

When Ngaia found out she was pregnant, she'd gone to Leo to argue her choices.

'You have no idea,' Leo said. 'The reality of my own life started folding in on me. It had been collapsing for a while, I know, but when she crumpled, so did I. When Ngaia talked about giving the baby away, I saw me. When she talked about the effort it would take to be a mother, I saw you. When she talked about Tineke as the only person she knew who might actually know what to do with a kid, I saw Jenny. When she talked about kids brought up by shitty parents I probably cried.

'I'd been thinking about trying to find you, since the first day I came back to New Zealand. Ngaia, all of eighteen, gave me such a bad time about it, told me I owed it to myself to at least bloody try. Said there could never be too much water under a bridge to wash it completely away, some dregs were always left, and I might even be surprised. I might even solve whatever the riddle was that was eating me. "You think about it," she said, as though I hadn't been doing that for years. But, supposing I tracked you down and you didn't want to know. Wouldn't that be worse?'

My God, Leo, yes. 'I understand.'

'In the end she decided to come out here to the coast, stay with Tineke. If Tineke was well and welcoming, she'd stay and have the baby, take it from there. She just needed someone she could count on staying put, she said, so she picked Tineke, who was too old to go anywhere, and then she organised me. Told me she'd heard about this bloke with a bach to rent, so if I wanted to get my own shit together, mellow out at the beach, the place was empty. I think you can blame your past for how your life is, up to a point, but after that it's up to you. It seemed a good idea. I packed up my flat and followed her out to the bay. It's been such a healing time, I still feel grateful to her. I don't think I changed her life as much as she changed mine.'

'Then Rick died and I found you by a strange twist of fate.'

'Yes,' he said. 'And it is strange, because now Ngaia has Tineke and the baby, and old Tineke has Ngaia and the baby. And then there's me and you, and we might actually be okay.'

'Sanctuary,' I said, 'this coast.'

As we stood in silence, I thought how the past had often thrown up walls too high, too wide, to climb. But as we headed slowly towards the Lake Onoke Park playground and its pair of wobbly swings, I thought how oddly easy it had been to find a ladder to climb.

Even if, here and there, rungs were missing.

'What happened between you and your father?'

I felt the tension in his body before I saw it. He stiffened, almost tripped, bent to pick up a stick to toss into the lagoon.

'Sometimes, I think I should write it all down,' he said quietly. 'Like a story that happened to someone else. Kind of deactivate it.'

I said gently, 'But it happened to you.'

'Yes, but in the great scheme of things, when you talk to kids like Ngaia and find out how and what they've been through…' His words ran out. He picked up another twig. 'And yet, really, it was so big it determined the rest of my life.'

Chapter Twenty-six

The boy was lonely, anybody could see, and Colleen knew it, too – probably all of Cooktown did. She might have brittle bones and a brittle temper to match but her heart was sound and knowing. She'd watched something follow the boy around since he'd got here, like a dark dangerous cloud, looking for a place to settle. All his little expressions – smiling, frowning, with tears – would appear, disappear, reappear, within the space of an hour. Lonely, yep, he was lonely, and a loner too – hard to know which came first. And she'd heard how the kids at school gave him hell for being an outsider who talked different, a bloody Kiwi. His father didn't want to listen when he tried to tell him how it was. Sometimes she stood up for him.

'He's the way he is. Had too much molly-coddling. Leave the kid alone.'

It wasn't that his father was bad with him, more he wasn't there. He treated the kid like an object, a suitcase he'd picked up and put down. He didn't abuse the boy, but he didn't understand him or seem to notice that his only friend was that old scar-faced dog called Soldier, named by some crazy old 'Nam vet because they both had cuts over their eye. That ratty dog had hung around Cooktown so long, no one knew who he belonged to now and no one cared.

She gave the boy scraps for Soldier and a water bowl.

It was hard for the boy when his father was around, worse when he was out at sea and even harder when he came back. There was always that unspoken trouble between them, like a question that never got asked.

The father was lucky to have her there when he took off in those leaky bloody boats, but he knew it, and paid his rent on time. He threw his money down on the table before waltzing himself into town on a Friday night, hoping to get drunk or laid.

The early mornings he made it back before her lights went out, he'd pretend to get lost on the way to the donger and pound loudly on her door, demand she get herself up and have a drink. Sometimes she did it, too, trying to solve the mystery of him and the boy, but all he'd do was tell fishing stories, over and over again.

The only time she'd seen the boy happy was when he was heading off to the wharf to go fishing.

'The barramundi,' the boy said, stretching his arms, 'big as baseball bats!'

Sometimes she went with him. Lately, he'd gone alone.

She'd watch him, not saying much, slipping breakfast to the dog. Then down the path with Soldier snuffling and coughing in the red dust.

The boy had been in Cooktown with Colleen for almost three years, when his father announced one morning that he'd finished with the prawn boats. Time to go, he said to the boy. Time for another adventure.

'What do you mean?' Colleen said, touching the boy on the back of the head.

'Got a job at the station at Laura,' the father said. 'Talking to the bloke at the Sovereign and he reckons there's a place for me and the kid.'

But Colleen looked in the boy's eyes and they were wary. This was something else, for him, not an adventure.

'Take the dog,' Colleen said.

At Laura, life was no better or worse, it simply changed. The boy did correspondence school, like the other kids on the ranch, and turned thirteen in the middle of nowhere. At fourteen he rode the land on a horse with the ranch hands, the dog at his feet. The sun burned his neck to a leathery red and he grew fit and lean, could have stepped into the boots of a cowboy, as easy as you please. Riding a horse made him feel bigger than any walking on the ground.

By the time he was fifteen, the schoolwork disappeared. The boy had become a stockman, relaxed in the saddle, in the company of men, at ease with them, black and white. But one night over a beer outside, his father announced, as flatly as he had those years before, that it was time to leave again, do something different. The boy had heard the bunkhouse talk, that his father was too long in the tooth, too hard to handle, that if he didn't leave soon of his own accord, someone would make him leave. The boy felt something crack inside him.

'Tom Price,' his father said. 'Out west. Mining work there.'

The boy found the place on the bunkhouse map. If Cooktown was the flea on the dog's ear, then Tom Price wasn't far from where its nose would be. He sat down beside Soldier and rubbed his jaw. From the map the boy had seen it would take more than a week to get there. Soldier could sit on the back of the ute. He'd rig him up some shade.

'Leaving first light tomorrow so pack your gear. And leave any thoughts of bringing that dirtbag behind in its kennel. I'm not having that thing breathing down my neck the whole way over.'

'I'm not leaving Soldier,' the boy said.

'Forget it.'

And he drew himself up for the first time, sighted his father as though down the barrel of a gun. He saw him for what he had become – just a sour old man, wearing a weather-beaten hat down low over a weather-beaten scowl. The eyes had kept their flinty stare.

'I'll come with you,' the boy said, 'if I have to, but I won't leave my dog.'

'Don't be barmy,' the father said. 'He's on his last legs anyway.'

It was true, the dog was old, but he was family. He'd heard every secret wish and whisper from before the boy was twelve. The father pulled in close enough for the boy to smell the beer on his breath, watch the lips pull back over neglected teeth. He wouldn't end up like him. He wasn't afraid, he'd never been less afraid in his life. He'd never been smacked around, his father had preferred words that hurt, phrases that flew like bats over the mangroves and landed inside your head. 'Mummy's boy, Mummy's little baby.'

'Get me a rifle and I'll shoot the bastard. Problem solved.'

'I'll shoot you first,' the boy said.

And how quickly it had happened, his father swinging into the ute and leaving. How easily he'd watched him drive away. He'd stared at the ute until it was nothing but a distant fly on an endless piece of cardboard.

How sensibly life had continued. How smoothly time had passed. How little he had missed him, staying on until the dog died, not by savage age, but by the bite of an unknown snake. By that time he was nineteen and had saved up some money.

Chapter Twenty-seven

Leo stopped talking, paused for breath, but my mind kept right on going, all the way across the Tasman Sea, where it wouldn't come back.

'And then? Then did the boy come home?'

'No,' Leo said. 'It was after the dog died that he found it hard. The boy drifted. He drifted round for years.'

'Did he ever go looking for his father?'

'No. But one day, sitting on a crowded beach in Perth, he decided to come home, back to New Zealand at least, maybe back to Pirongia, back to the old house, maybe back to the Marakopa Beach.'

'How old was the boy then?'

'Coming up twenty-four.' And for the first time since he'd started his story, Leo switched from the third person and began talking about himself.

'It's not as though it was the first time I'd thought of coming back, but I'd gone over there on Rick's passport, and since then the laws had changed, and anyway, he'd kept his passport, so I was stuck with no papers, a new identity and no birth certificate. I used to chew it over sometimes, how I'd manage to get back, supposing I wanted badly enough to come. In the end it was simpler than I thought. I had a mate and we weren't too different, met him on the rodeo circuit.' He gave me an small odd smile, as though he wasn't sure if he should be proud or ashamed of it.

'He was a rider while I was just a hand. Anyway, I cut my hair to match his, and grew a beard to match the photo and I travelled back to New Zealand on his passport. Sent it back to him once I landed, though God only knows what he could have done with it, with its stamp into New Zealand and none out. Actually, that still makes me laugh.'

We were at the Onoke Park swings. I dropped my dragging butt in one.

'When I got to Pirongia the house was no longer there, pulled down to make way for a big new farmhouse. Without it, I just couldn't stay.'

Leo lifted his shoulders, dropped them down, as if to say, I don't know why, but there you go, nothing was the same. 'It was a good life there, wasn't it?' There was something plaintive and childlike in his tone, as though, without me to agree with him, all his memories might turn to ashes.

'Yes, it was a good life.' Fresh bread, a surplus of eggs, books, games and fun. Jenny to keep us afloat.

He seemed to regain his equilibrium and leaned back in his swing. His hair fell down his back.

'So off I went to Wellington, convinced that it was an omen, the house being gone, a sign to put the old stuff to rest. For a while it almost worked. Student loan, went to tech, trying to catch up on the learning I thought I'd missed growing up where I did. It was a good thought, but crazy, really. I was no longer a kid. Half the time I felt pretty removed from it. But it was something, it was a start. In the end I did an English paper and got the job teaching adult literacy to people aged sixteen to fifty-nine.'

His chin went a little way into the air.

'We always said that with a little pride, where I worked. I think I was good at it too. Well, for a while.'

I believed him. I could see him as he'd been with Ngaia, empathetic, non-judging. I thought again how keen he'd been to listen to people and their stories as a child. He'd make a good teacher.

'But then everything began to fall apart, as I said, and I ended up here in the bay as some sort of unpaid midwife to Ngaia. Not that I minded. I think Ngaia saved my life.'

And life is full of fearsome parallels. Up in Auckland, my

grip on things had been slipping, while at the opposite end of the island, Leo's grip had been loosening too. I knew that what he was telling me was only half of it, that his desperation must have run far deeper than he'd let on. I knew from experience you could outrun things that were meant to kill you. But I also knew you might survive the initial stages, only to die slowly later from a very old wound.

It's the way of wounds. After a while they grow flat, lie down. But just because they're no longer visible, doesn't mean they're not there.

I knew what Leo wasn't saying – that he'd been very close to the edge.

We hung on the swings, side by side.

'So, how about you,' Leo asked. 'What's your story?'

I took a deep breath but somehow a miracle had occurred. I knew I could give it all up, every last gory detail.

I held Leo's hand as I spoke, for his comfort and not mine.

'I couldn't believe you were never coming back. I never believed it. I was sure it was all going to be one of those big huge mistakes, you know, where people go out in a boat and turn up in a different harbour after a hundred days or more. Except, of course, there was no boat, no distant shore, no rescue. Even after I knew Rick had taken you to Sydney, I thought maybe he'd change his mind. That he'd bring you back when the novelty of keeping you wore off.'

Leo flinched. I squeezed his hand. 'Sorry.'

'Don't be, Mum. I think that's exactly what happened. The novelty wore off, but by then it was too late. The deed was done. Stupid pride would have got in Rick's way, prevented him coming back. It would have meant getting in touch with you and it would have all got too hard for him to deal with, I think.'

He scuffed up a small cloud of sand with his feet. 'Also, you know, I think about this a lot, and I think it's why his resentment built up and consumed him. I think I cost him more than he'd imagined. Oh, not in dollars, but in not being able to ever come back. He loved New Zealand.'

'But he did come back, in the end.'

'Yes, but after how many years? Enough about Rick. Tell me about Jenny.'

Yes, I could do this too.

'Jenny died not long after you went, almost within the year.'

And how I'd yelled and screamed and hated her for copping out, for leaving me alone to do it by myself. I'd been the one who had prayed to die. How dare she get there first!

'I borrowed on the house to pay someone, an old ex-policeman to find you. Turned out he wasn't much of a policeman. He was a crook.'

I felt my old frustration rise up and fill my lungs like acrid smoke. I'd been so naïve. I trusted anyone who put their hand up to help, anyone who offered fast results for not much money.

'Simon Taylor had a motto: take the money and run. Deal with the fallout later. He strung me along for months and months, and then he took my money and stayed behind in Sydney.'

I fell silent for a time, remembering how little I'd had left, nothing in the way of money or a future. Somehow I'd managed to keep bobbing above the water, but it dawned on me, talking about it now, that I could even see an upside.

'I went to Grant who ran the bank in Te Kuiti. He kept in touch, ringing me up, making suggestions, asking for progress reports. Some days he'd say, "Go outside, Cassie, go for a walk, smell the sunshine, do not hide away inside. Go out and feed those chickens, go kick some thistles about." Well, let's just say that some days, if not for Grant, I wouldn't have made it out of bed.'

Before long he'd started calling. 'Get dressed, I've brought your lunch.'

'He would arrive with sandwiches from the bakery, or a couple of sticky buns. "Eat," he would tell me. "You must eat."'

And I'd follow his orders as though he was the father I'd never known.

I plucked at my wedding ring, turned it round and round. What that the reason it had started?

'He couldn't do anything to find you, but he was there and he helped.'

'And you fell in love, got married, and had a couple of kids, the whole romantic picture.' How simple he made that sound.

'Yes. But not quite as effortlessly as that.'

I stopped twisting the ring and looked at Leo. 'Can I ask you? Do you mind too much?'

They were only kids, props in a stage play they knew nothing about. But they had never filled the hole inside me, never right to the top. I needed them to be something they could never be – they could never be Leo.

It was me who looked away first.

'Grant seems a decent bloke.'

'Yes, he is. And he feels more for you than you could guess, because he knows the story. But Ty and Charity don't know. I've never told them.'

'So,' Leo said. 'I'm your secret?'

'Not a secret, no. A private memory. With all of you gone, it's all I had left that belonged to me. I didn't think they had to know.'

'How old did you say they were? Fifteen and sixteen?'

I nodded.

'I would have thought they'd be old enough now, no matter what the details. Who's going to tell them?'

I knew immediately I'd want Grant to do it. Go in as smoothly as Jenny's marble rolling pin and smooth away the lumps.

Chapter Twenty-eight

We were almost back to the hotel.

'Hey, pilgrims!' Matt stood outside the main doors, flapping a tea-towel like someone's maid.

'Perfect timing! Dinner's ready. The new mother has to eat.'

'How is she?' Leo and I said both at once. 'How's Tauho Iti?'

'He's fantastic,' Matt said. 'Haven't heard him cry once. I thought that's what babies do, they cry all the time.'

'Not all of them,' I said. 'Not the lucky ones who have had a special birth.'

'I thought you said he was a big baby,' Matt said. 'He's not, he's bloody little. Makes you just want to run away with him and hide him from the world.'

'I think he will be safe out here, away from the world, for a while,' Leo said.

I was lost in a fog of optimism, little Pollyanna, picturing Tauho Iti in a year, maybe two, running through the dunes while Tineke leaned on her honeysuckle stick, while, beside her, Ngaia ballooned with pride.

'He is big. I know from experience that baby must weigh in at nearly ten pounds.'

'The old woman's acting really weird,' Matt said. 'Like she's been eating magic mushrooms. Her eyes are all over the place and she can't stop smirking. And your husband doesn't seem normal either, Prophet, I have to say, packing himself off into the King Country wilderness to do the right thang. And of course, my heart's broken,' he continued, draping the tea-towel over his heart. 'My heart's broken

153

completely into pieces.' He shut one eye and opened the other. 'Is this the right side?'

'Unless you're some kind of mutant, yes, it is.'

'Well, like I said, I'm heartbroken. Everyone's planning to leave except Laurel.' He drawled dramatically. 'But far out, I intend to live long enough to be a hero. I'm about to dish up dinner for six. Six and a half if you count the baby, and you leave Laurel and Hardy out.'

'Don't tell me,' I said. 'Fish and chips with parsley.'

'On a special day like this? Are you mad? Fish and chips and eggs.'

He ushered us into the dining room, where someone had shoved two tables together, covered them in a white and yellow cloth and spaced out five chairs. Salt, vinegar and tomato sauce watched over the knives and forks, along with a strange floral wreath. I wandered over to see what it was made of and found seaweed, pine needles and wood.

'I want credit for that,' Matt said. 'A genuine artistic Lake Ferry centrepiece. I put the paua shell in the middle. Don't worry, I washed it first.'

Tineke, as if by divine right, sat down at the head of the table, where she began tapping her cane impatiently on the floor.

'Come on, come on,' she said. 'What yous fullas doing? This old girl's hungry. Let's eat.'

I watched Grant drag one of the worn armchairs in from the bar, placing it precisely up to the table and next to the window. He guided the new mother into her throne, wrapped a blanket around her knees, and tucked the baby up with an inch of scalp showing. Leo went over and touched the baby's head.

Then Matt arrived, carrying a tray of sandwiches. 'Dinner is about to be served.'

Don't worry, Prophet,' he said, when he saw my face, 'These are merely the appetisers. Tuna, and still under the heading of fish.'

And then in a loud aside to Leo he said. 'I know. The biggest insult to a fisherman is to offer him some from a can but, mate, you were too busy today to catch us a fresh one.'

The rest of us took our seats, sitting down where Matt ordered us to, Grant at the opposite end from Tineke, me next to Leo on the side that faced the window. Matt pulled Ngaia's royal seat up closer, but it was so low, she seemed to be sitting on the floor. He ran off to a bedroom to fetch pillows to prop her up. When he was finished, he sat down in the last empty chair beside her.

I began to pour water into glasses as though it was the most exquisite wine.

'I propose a toast,' I said.

'I could bring you some real stuff. Hard liquor,' Matt said.

'No,' I said in a gush. 'Don't you dare.'

'Ahem,' Grant said, standing up, taking charge. 'This has got to be done properly so I will do it.' He raised a glass. 'Here is to life and death and taxes,' he joked.

'Forgive me. I will start again. Here is to life and death and little babies. New beginnings, final endings and things that never change. Here's to being lost and found. Here's to the future and burying the past.'

'Yes, to Rick,' I said loudly.

'Now, now, Prophet,' Matt said.

'Don't call me that,' I said. 'I never saw this portent in my life.'

For the second time at the Lake Ferry, I ate fish and chips. Then Leo stood up and pushed his hair behind his ears. 'My turn. Here's to Tineke who never hesitated to hold out her hand, who offered her house to both these poor little orphans.'

To which Ngaia said, 'Hear, hear.'

'To Ngaia who by-passed the entire medical profession to have her baby on the floor of this old pub. To those who cooked the dinner.'

It would have been enough.

'And here's to Mum.'

After the food was gone and Leo and Grant were doing the dishes like a couple of experienced kitchen hands, I went to find Matt the cook, to thank him. For some of us he'd provided not only a last supper, but an absolute first. I knew I'd find him out the back on the leeward side, pulling hard on a cigarette. When I sat down beside him on the step he tried his best to sound philosophical.

'Ever wondered what's over them there hills?'

'Gold, of course. There's gold in them thar hills."

'Good. That's where I'm going then, to look for gold,' Matt said. 'It's time I was leaving too.'

'Where will you go?'

'I'm not sure. Somewhere. Nowhere. Away. It's time I got out from under Laurel's thumb. I've decided I'm going to take off this time, before she does another runner. I'm going to out-runner her.'

How strange, that one person's retreat could be another person's trap.

He said, 'Remember that first day out here on the steps?'

'Was it only a week ago?'

'You said I should take a trip around the world.'

I nodded. 'Hmm.'

'Well, that's kinda what I'm thinking, maybe not the whole world exactly but maybe I'll stick a toe in and test. I'll head for the South Island. I think I'll go looking for my father.'

He played with his cigarette packet, turning it over and over in his hands.

'Thanks for making me part of all this, Prophet. It sort of restores my faith in family, to tell the truth.'

I thought of all our confused connections. Leo's, Grant's. Ngaia's, the baby. Matt's and mine.

'We're not really a family.'

'Aren't you? Today, around the table, you looked like a family to me. You have an extended whanau now, you know, whether you wanted one or not.'

I wondered how Tineke would feel about that. Maybe she wouldn't mind. I chucked Charity and Ty into the mix. I knew he was right.

We sat for a while, saying nothing.

'Will you be all right?' I asked him. 'This thing between us…' I didn't know what to call it. 'You had me worried for a while, that you'd tell Grant…'

'Listen, Prophet, the closest thing I get to a shag around here is the squawky variety that sits on a rock. Do you think I'd jeopardise my chances for a repeat performance?' But then he was suddenly serious, making certain I'd understand. 'You never had anything to fear from me, I should have told you that. But, for what it's worth, the time with you meant a lot. I think, because you were less than perfect…' He was about to rephrase, but changed his mind. 'Because you were less perfect, it somehow made everything more real, more intimate, less casual, if you know what I mean.'

'Yes.' It had been the same for me. He'd taken a bird with a broken wing and smoothed out all her joints.

'So what do you think, Prophet? Will I be all right?'

'Yes. I think, if we're very lucky, everyone will be all right.'

He beamed at something invisible.

'Far out, it was awful watching you squirm, when I had no intention of dobbing you in to Grant or anyone else. I only ever wished you well, Prophet. I only ever wished you well.'

I stood up to go. 'One last kiss for auld lang syne?'

I offered my cheek but he turned my head and kissed me on the mouth.

Chapter Twenty-nine

Grant was preparing to go too. We stood alone between the Beemers. 'Stay as long as you like, Cassie. I will ring after the funeral and tell you what it was like. Stay until you are absolutely certain you are ready to come home. Do not worry about the kids, I will see that they are fine. I will even take Charity shopping. For the ball dress,' he explained.

'Bring Leo with you but only if he wants to come. You cannot assume anything, Cassie, not yet. Take your time. Ask questions. Listen to his answers. Do not fill in any of his spaces yourself. Tell Leo I hope to see him soon. I would like your eldest son to show me how to catch fish.'

'God, Grant, what would I do without you?'

'I hope we never find out.' He wiped his hand across his brow. 'Cassie, promise me only good things will happen to us now.' Then his worry subsided a little, not fully, but enough. 'Not necessarily only good things, I am not that unrealistic, but between you and me. I always knew there was enough there to make it all worthwhile, but there have been times when you were so distant, I've felt so afraid. Somehow,' he finished, 'you are different here.'

'Yes, I'm different here.'

I'm different, I wanted to say, because finding Leo has changed me. Different because of Matt and an act of such grace and stupidity that it could have compromised us all. But because of it, I see how much I want to keep you.

I'm different because Rick is dead and the past can be put to bed. Perhaps not entirely but the weight of it has shifted. And while my heart isn't big or open enough for forgiveness, I at least have some small insight into why Rick might have done what he did. I see the part I might have played. I also see that some of the responsibility might be mine. And Jenny's.

But I didn't get to say any of this because Grant put his arms around me and held me so tight against his chest I couldn't breathe.

In the end, I thumped him.

'Ouch,' Grant said as he let me go. 'Here comes Leo to say goodbye. You know, Cassie, he seems a fine boy. A fine man.'

'Yes,' I thought, 'this bay is full of them.'

'Before I forget, any messages for Beth Conaglen?'

I shook my head. I'd be in touch. One day I might tell Beth I'd given up my Polly Filler job. Maybe over coffee on some neutral ground.

Grant said, 'What would you like me to tell the kids?'

'All of it.'

'I will tell them some of it, Cassie. But the rest you will need to tell them yourself. There is so much only you and Leo know.'

'Yes, you're right.' There was a lot I hadn't yet told Grant, things I'd learnt today on a swing in the Lake Onoke playground.

'You can fill us all in together,' he said. 'All at once. How does that sound?'

'Sounds good.' Sounds like someone's got her old job back, already.

Then Leo arrived beside us in a pair of borrowed jeans and an Export Gold t-shirt.

'Mine were a bit mucky. I'll have to remember to tell Ngaia. Giving birth might be natural but it's not at all like gutting fish.'

I stopped holding onto Grant and went to Leo instead. It was as though I was the child and he was the parent who would keep me on the ground. I felt he was some marvellous kite that might be whisked away in a moment, to soar out over the waves. I wrapped an invisible string around my wrist and tied it to him. But loosely, loosely, Cass.

'Take care,' Leo said, as he shook Grant's hand.

'We will meet again soon.'

Then Grant kissed me in a perfectly perfunctory fashion, climbed into his BMW and wound down the window. 'You know, Cassie, I never knew how pretentious matching cars look. Particularly the red ones. Flip you for which one we keep and which one we sell.'

And then he was gone.

As his car spun down the Lake Ferry road, I was overwhelmed by the feeling that I was standing inside a dream.

Leo put a hand out to steady me. 'Don't tell me you're crying.'

'I don't cry,' I lied.